Archie's®

BIG BOOK

VOLUME 3: ROCK 'N' ROLL

Publisher / Co-CEO: Jon Goldwater
Co-CEO: Nancy Silberkleit
Co-President / Editor-In-Chief: Victor Gorelick
Co-President: Mike Pellerito
Co-President: Alex Segura
Chief Creative Officer: Roberto Aguirre-Sacasa
Chief Operating Officer: William Mooar
Chief Financial Officer: Robert Wintle
Director of Book Sales & Operations: Jonathan Betancourt
Production Manager: Stephen Oswald
Lead Designer: Kari McLachlan
Associate Editor: Carlos Antunes
Assistant Editor / Proofreader: Jamie Lee Rotante

Published by Archie Comic Publications, Inc. 629 Fifth Avenue, Suite 100, Pelham, NY 10803-1242

ISBN: 978-1-68255-909-3

WRITTEN BY

Frank Doyle, George Gladir, Bill Golliher, Hal Lifson, Dick Malmgren, Dan Parent and Alex Simmons

ART BY

Bob Bolling, John Costanza, Doug Crane, Jon D'Agostino, Dan DeCarlo, Dan DeCarlo Jr., Marty Epp, Holly G!, Stan Goldberg, Bill Golliher, Barry Grossman, Rich Koslowski, Rudy Lapick, Harry Lucey, Richard Maurizio, Jack Morelli, Al Nickerson, Rod Ollerenshaw, Dan Parent, Rosario "Tito" Peña, Fernando Ruiz, Bob Smith, Jane Smith Fisher, Chic Stone, Bill Vigoda, Glenn Whitmore, Bill Yoshida and Digikore Studios

COVER ART BY Dan Parent and Dan DeCarlo

Archie's BIG

TABLE OF CONTENTS

CHAPTER ONE THE 1960s

CHAPTER TWO THE 1970s

Archie's® BIG

INTRODUCTION

Archie, Betty, Veronica, Jughead and Reggie are ready to ROCK OUT! And it's no surprise—they've been doing it for over fifty years!

The Archies band was originally created as part of Filmation's *The Archie Show* which ran on CBS from September 1968 to August 1969. On the show, the friends appeared as a garage rock/bubblegum pop band that featured Archie on lead guitar. The Archies' music was recorded by real-life session musicians. Their most famous song is "Sugar, Sugar," which went to number one on the pop chart in 1969, sold millions of copies, and was awarded a gold disc. It was also ranked as the *Billboard* Hot 100 No. 1 song of that year, the only time a fictional band has ever claimed the coveted top spot!

It only makes sense that this fame made its way into the comics as well! Stories featuring the band have continued throughout the decades since its inception, including an all-new series on sale now that sees The Archies team-up with real-world musical acts like the RAMONES, BLONDIE, and even bubblegum pop counterparts THE MONKEES!

This Big Book collection highlights some of the best classic rock 'n' roll stories featuring The Archies throughout their publishing history, with a few added bonuses including unforgettable Josie and the Pussycats stories, and even a few Sabrina the Teenage music/magic mash-ups!

So turn your amps up to 11 and rock on with Archie and the gang!

CHAPTER ONE

The 1960s

THE ARCHIES IN
LABOR OF LOVE
APRIL 1968

SCRIPT: FRANK DOYLE PENCILS: DAN DECARLO
INKS: RUDY LAPICK LETTERS: BILL YOSHIDA

THE ARCHIES IN
MUSIC SOOTHES
SEPTEMBER 1968

SCRIPT: FRANK DOYLE PENCILS: HARRY LUCEY
INKS: MARTY EPP LETTERS: BILL YOSHIDA

THE Archies IN "LABOR of LOVE"
THE ARCHIE GROUP, LIKE CHICKEN SOUP, WILL CURE WHATEVER AILS YA! OUR SONGS ARE LOUD, WE PLEASE THE CROWD, OUR MUSIC NEVER FAILS YA!
GOOD GRIEF!
SLURP!
THE ARC

ALL RIGHT! COOL IT, BOYS! PUT A LID ON IT!

CAN'T YOU SEE I'VE GOT A CUSTOMER? EVERYBODY DOESN'T DIG THAT RACKET!

I DO! IN FACT, I'D LIKE TO HIRE THEM!
YOU WANT TO BREAK A LEASE?

I MANAGE THE ROVING EYE DISCOTHEQUE!
BINGO!

BETTY! VERONICA! DID YOU HEAR THAT? WE'VE GOT A BOOKING!
WONDERFUL, ARCHIEKINS! WE'LL HAVE SO MUCH FUN, SPENDING YOUR SALARY!!
YOU CAN START TONIGHT! I'LL BOUNCE THOSE SOUNDLESS SLOBS I'VE GOT NOW!
2

MAN! WE'RE REALLY PACKING THEM IN!
THERE'S NO BIZ LIKE SHOW BIZ!
THE ROVING EYE

HEY! IT'S THE ARCHIES!
PLUG IN AND GIVE OUT, GUYS!

YOU'D BETTER BE GOOD! WE HAD TO PAY TO HEAR YOU TONIGHT!

OH, BILLIE JO, I LOVED YA SO, I FELT SO MUCH ALIVE, SO TELL ME WHY YA HAD TO GO AN' TAKE THAT AWFUL DIVE?
3

HEY! HEY, ARCH! SMARTEN UP! YOU MISSED YOUR CUE!

HYUK! THE OL' REDHEAD IS TURNING PURPLE WATCHING RONNIE AND THE BOSS!

HOW LONG HAVE YOU HAD THAT BEE TATTOOED ON YOUR FACE?
IT'S A DECAL, LONG-SNOOT! IT'S THE LATEST THING!

SEE? BETTY'S GOT ONE, TOO!
WHAT'S THE WORLD COMING TO?

WHY DOESN'T THAT JOKER LEAVE MY GIRL ALONE AND GO TEND TO BUSINESS?
STICK TO YOUR STRUMMIN', SUCKER! THAT'S WHAT'S BRINGING IN THE BREAD!
4

ARCH! WHAT ARE YOU DOING?
DON'T BOTHER ME!

TWANG!
OUCH!
WAP

I'VE BEEN STUNG! IT FELT LIKE A BEE, OR...

...THERE IT IS!
SLAP!
BOOM!
5

MAN! RIGHT ON THE TATTOO!
WE'D BETTER TAKE FIVE!!

YOU BOYS SOUND GREAT!
I DIDN'T THINK YOU WERE LISTENING!

HEY! LOOK!
IT'S THE CASHIER!
GET THAT GAG OUT OF HER MOUTH!
MMMPH!..SNKLFT... BRRRTZZ!!!

ROBBED! WE'VE BEEN ROBBED! A MASKED HOOD STOLE ALL THE MONEY!!

HOW MUCH DID HE GET?
AT LEAST EIGHT HUNDRED DOLLARS!
WHAT'D HE LOOK LIKE?
6

MAN, HE WAS WEARING THE CRAZIEST SET OF THREADS!
LIKE WHAT?

INDESCRIBABLE!
WAIT! I'LL DRAW A PICTURE!

THERE! ISN'T THAT THE WILDEST OUTFIT?

HMPH! SOME KIND OF EXHIBITIONIST!

HE OUGHTTA BE EASY TO CATCH!
SURE! HE'LL STICK OUT LIKE A SORE THUMB IN THAT RIG!
7

HE ALSO HAD AN ARROW TATTOO ON HIS WRIST!
WHAT GOOD IS THAT?
FL

THOSE TATTOOS ARE DECALS! THEY CAN BE REMOVED!
REGGIE'S RIGHT!

HEY!
PART OF THE EIGHT HUNDRED WAS OUR PAY!

T-U-F, BOYS! THAT'S HOW THE OL' BALL BOUNCES!

THIS OUTFIT'S BEEN MAKING A MINT! YOU CAN STILL AFFORD TO PAY US!
YEAH! WE DEMAND OUR SALARY!
OUT! CRUMBS! WE'RE CLOSING UP FOR THE NIGHT!
8

MAN! I'D LIKE TO GET MY HANDS ON THE CROOK WHO STOLE OUR DOUGH!
ALL THAT WORK FOR NOTHING!
THE ROVING EYE

WOULD YOU LIKE TO KNOW WHO HAS ALL YOUR MONEY?
YOU KNOW?

THAT MANAGER FLASHED A TATTOO OF AN ARROW ON HIS WRIST WHILE WE WERE DANCING! A REAL ONE!

WHY, THAT CREEP! HE'S ROBBING THE OWNER OF THE DISCO!
DISGUISED IN THAT SQUARE JOHN OUTFIT, NOBODY KNEW HIM!

HE'LL BE TAKING THE MONEY HOME WITH HIM! WHAT SAY WE WAIT?
WHO'S GOING?

HYUK! NOT BAD FOR A NIGHT'S WORK! AN EIGHT HUNDRED DOLLAR BONUS!
9

AND THE STUPID OWNER IS INSURED, SO IT'S NO LOSS TO HIM!

THE BEAUTY PART IS, NOBODY EVER SUSPECTS THE MANAGER OF KNOCKIN' OVER HIS OWN JOINT!

WHOOPS
ER-WHAT THAT IS THERE, MISTER, IS GREASE IN WHICH YOU'RE SLIPPIN'!

THE GREASE! IT CAME FROM THE BUCKET IN WHICH YOUR FOOT IS NOW JAMMED!
SPLOOSH!

YOU!...YOU GREASED THAT STEP, YOU...

EEYURK!!
SPLAT
WHOOSH!
10

MY! MY! DO LOOK AT ALL THAT MONEY! I DO BELIEVE THIS BEARS INVESTIGATING!
SOB

AS OWNER OF THE ROVING EYE, I OWE YOU BOYS A DEBT OF GRATITUDE! NAME YOUR OWN REWARD!

OH, WE'RE NOT RICH, BUT WE'RE NOT GREEDY, AND WE MAY LOOK A TRIFLE SEEDY! BUT LET US PLAY AND WE'RE NOT NEEDY, FOR THIS IS LIVIN', YES INDEEDY!
AMAZING! THE ONLY REWARD THEY WANTED WAS A CHANCE TO WORK!
THERE'S A LOT MORE TO THE ARCHIES THAN MEETS THE EYE, MISTER!
THE ARCHIES
THE END

THE Archies in Music SOOTHES
BAYBEH, KISS ME HARD 'N' FAST, HOL' ME TIGHT AN' MAKE IT LAST, LOVE IS ALL AN' ALL IS LOVE, IT TURNS A HAWK INTO A DOVE
IT'S NOT THAT I DON'T LOVE THESE OLD CLASSICS, BUT MY TEETH ARE BEGINNING TO RATTLE!
AND I JUST PUT A CAKE IN THE OVEN!
1

THIS IS SNEAKY, BUT IT'S BETTER THAN HURTING THEIR FEELINGS!
FUSE BOX

HEY! THE AMPS HAVE GONE DEAD!
WE HAVE NO JUICE!
The Archies

BLOWN FUSE, BOYS! ... AND I DON'T HAVE A SPARE!
I'LL BE BACK WITH A NEW ONE IN AN HOUR OR SO!

AN HOUR WILL COOL THE CREATIVE SPARK!
OH?
SORRY, POP! ... WE CAN'T WAIT!

A FINE GROUP OF BOYS! ... AND EXCELLENT MUSICIANS! .... I THINK!
WHY DO THEY ALWAYS PLAY, ... "MUSIC TO BREAK EARDRUMS BY?"
2

HALT! I APPRECIATE MUSIC AS MUCH AS THE NEXT MAN!
POP'S
CHOCKLIT
SHOP

...BUT THAT STUFF YOU GAVE OUT LAST TIME CURDLED MY CREAM!

WE'RE LIVING IN A CULTURAL DESERT!
ALL CREATIVITY STIFLED BY THE ESTAB-LISHMENT!
YOU'RE MOVING ME TO TEARS!

BUT YOU'RE NOT MOVING INSIDE MY SHOP WITH THOSE NOISEMAKERS!
HEY! WHY DON'T WE PLAY OUT HERE?

ARE YOU NUTS? WHO CAN MAKE MUSIC WITHOUT ELECTRICITY?
I FORGOT!
NO PROBLEM!

I HAVE A LONG EXTENSION CORD!
YOU MEAN WE CAN PLUG IN ON YOUR JUICE?
3

YOU'RE ALL HEART, POPS!
THAT'S KIND OF YOU, ARCHIE! ACTUALLY, THOUGH, I'M ALMOST ALL FLAB!

OKAY! NOW HIT IT! A-ONE, A-TWO...
The Archies

WHAT A LOVELY FEELING!...TO BE ABLE TO TURN DOWN THE VOLUME JUST BY CLOSING THE DOOR!
OOOH! IT'S THE STREET WHERE WE MEET AND LAY ON THAT BEAT.. IT'S THE SIDEWALK SERENA-ADE
HOPPE

WHIRR!
WHAT THE...?

ZOOM!
4

THANKS, POPS! ... BUT THIS IS TOO DANGEROUS!
POP'S
CHOCKLIT
SHOP

WHY DON'T YOU PRACTICE AT MY HOUSE?
BETTY! ... YOU ARE A TRUE PATRON OF THE ARTS!

ISN'T IT GROOVY, MOM? THE ARCHIES ARE GOING TO PLAY RIGHT HERE! ... IN OUR HOUSE!
URK!

IT'S, LIKE, TOO MUCH! EEEE! I CAN BARELY STAND IT!
FUNNY! ALMOST THE VERY WORDS I WOULD HAVE USED!

POPPER DOPPER TEENY BOPPER EENY MEENY MINEY MO! PHONEY BONEY, MACARONI. GO, MAN, GO!
EEP!
5

ER... ARCHIE!...THERE'S JUST NO MEETING OF THE MINDS WITH THE OLDER GENERATION!
I'M AFRAID MOM'S ABOUT TO LOWER THE BOOM!

HAVING LOVE IN OUR HEARTS DOESN'T MEAN NO SMARTS IN OUR HEADS, BETS!
LEAVE THIS TO THE ARCHIES!

OH, SHE'S KINDLY AND GENTLE, SHE'S JUST SUPER DUPER!... IF YOU HAD HER YOU'D WANT FOR NO OTHER! THE BEST OF THE BEST IS OUR OWN, MRS. COOPER, THE EXQUISITE MODEL OF MOTHER!
The Archies

WHAT? I CAN'T HEAR YOU ABOVE THAT DIN!
I SAID, AREN'T THEY GROOVY? ...JUST TOO MUCH! I COULD LISTEN TO THEM ALL NIGHT!
THE END
6

CHAPTER TWO

The 1970s

THE ARCHIES IN
MISTER APPETITE
JUNE 1970

SCRIPT: FRANK DOYLE PENCILS: HARRY LUCEY INKS: MARTY EPP

THE ARCHIES IN
REGGIE MANTLE, SUPER STAR
APRIL 1972

SCRIPT: DICK MALMGREN PENCILS: BOB BOLLING INKS: JON D'AGOSTINO
LETTERS: BILL YOSHIDA COLORS: BARRY GROSSMAN

THE ARCHIES IN
BUBBLE TROUBLE
AUGUST 1972

SCRIPT: GEORGE GLADIR PENCILS: BILL VIGODA
INKS: CHIC STONE LETTERS: BILL YOSHIDA

THE ARCHIES IN
GROUP GRIPE
FEBRUARY 1976

SCRIPT: GEORGE GLADIR PENCILS: HARRY LUCEY
LETTERS: BILL YOSHIDA COLORS: BARRY GROSSMAN

THE Archies in MISTER APPETITE

OKAY, TRIBE! LET'S RUN THROUGH NUMBERS SIX, SEVENTEEN, AND TWENTY! WE'RE A LITTLE WEAK ON THOSE!

SPEAK FOR YOURSELF, MIGHTY LEADER!... MANTLE IS EXCELLENT AT *EVERYTHING!*

The Archies

OH, THAT JUGGIE! ALWAYS SQUIRRELING THINGS AWAY!
REG!... JUG!... COME BACK! WE'VE GOT TO PRACTICE FOR TONIGHT'S DANCE!
IF I CATCH YOU YOU'LL HAVE FRUIT SALAD COMING OUT OF YOUR EARS!
DON'T BRUISE THE PEACHES!

HOW CAN HE RUN SO FAST WITH ALL THE FOOD HE PACKS AWAY?

WHAM!

ANYBODY EVER TELL YOU IT'S IMPOLITE TO EAT AND RUN?... ESPECIALLY IN MY HALLS!

IT WAS JUGHEAD'S FAULT, SIR!... BLAME HIM!
REALLY?
2

WE ARCHIES WERE ALL SET FOR A NICE PRACTICE SESSION AND OL' TROUBLE-MAKER JUG STARTS...
YOU MEAN YOUR DRUMMER ?
BIPPITY! BOOM! BOOM!
The Archies

HUH ? B-BUT HE WAS JUST TEARING THROUGH THE HALLS AND...
HMMM !
TZING!

WHY DON'T YOU STOP TRYING TO GET INNOCENT PEOPLE INTO TROUBLE ?
...AND YOU'RE HOLDING UP PRACTICE !
GRRRR!

FINE !... NOW ISN'T THAT MORE FUN THAN MAKING TROUBLE FOR YOUR FRIENDS ?

OH, I'M GONNA GET YOU ! OH-H-H HOW I'M GONNA GET EVEN !
3

WHAT THE ?... I THOUGHT I GOT ALL THAT FRUIT OUT!
RATTLE! RATTLE!

OOPS!... ONE MISERABLE GRAPE, I MISSED!

PLOK!
PING!

YOU JUST DON'T KNOW WHEN TO QUIT, DO YOU, REGGIE?
MR. WEATHERBEE! IT'S NOT MY FAULT!

IT'S THAT JUGHEAD! HE PUT THE FOOD IN MY GUITAR!
NOW I KNOW THAT'S NONSENSE!

JUGHEAD NEVER PUTS FOOD INTO ANYTHING BUT JUGHEAD!
4

YOU'RE COMING TO THE END OF YOUR ROPE, BOY!... WATCH IT!

GRRR.!... JUGHEAD AND HIS BOTTOMLESS STOMACH! HE'LL TURN THE WHOLE PLANET INTO A GARBAGE D...

..UMP!
ZWIP!

MY BANANA!... YOU RUINED MY BANANA!

NO! NO! BREAK IT UP!
TAKE FIVE! COOL IT!

I'LL TAKE A WALK TO COOL OFF! I THINK I'LL GO TO THE CAFETERIA AND GRAB A SMALL SNACK!
BRING ME SOME NICE, RICH, GOOEY DESERT, DARLING!
5

I DON'T KNOW HOW I CAN EVEN LOOK AT FOOD AFTER ALL THE TROUBLE IT CAUSED ME TODAY!
CAFETERIA

BUMP!

ALL OF YOUR LITTLE JESTS TODAY SEEM TO HAVE FOOD AS THEIR CENTRAL THEME!
YOU'RE TRYING TO BUG POOR JUGHEAD, AREN'T YOU ?

ONE MORE LITTLE FOOD GAG, BOY, AND YOU'VE HAD IT!... NOW LAY OFF JUGHEAD AND GET ON WITH YOUR PRACTICING!
IS THAT SMOKE COMING OUT OF HIS EARS ?
I DO BELIEVE HE'S OVERWROUGHT!
TZING! TZING! TZING!
The Archies
THE END

The Archies in "REGGIE MANTLE, SUPER STAR"
HEY, FELLOWS! HERE'S OUR CHANCE TO BREAK INTO THE MOVIES!
HUH ? WHY DO YOU WANT TO SNEAK INTO THE MOVIES ? DON'T YOU HAVE ANY MONEY ?
I'M NOT TALKING ABOUT THE THEATRE, DUMMY! MISTER STARFINDER IS IN TOWN!
WHO IS MISTER STARFINDER ?
HE'S A MOVIE TALENT SCOUT AND HE'S HERE IN RIVERDALE!
1

THEY SAY HE'S LOOKING FOR SOME KIDS TO PLAY PARTS IN A NEW MOVIE ABOUT THE YOUTH OF TODAY! THEY'RE GIVING SCREEN TESTS DOWN AT THE T.V. STUDIO!
THAT'S GREAT, REGGIE! WE'LL GO DOWN AND SEE IF WE CAN GET AN AUDITION!
The Archies
ARE YOU FLAKY, MAN? ALL THE TEEN-AGE YOUTH OF RIVERDALE WILL BE AT THAT T.V. STUDIO!
WE HAVE TO BEAT THEM ALL TO THE PUNCH, AND I KNOW JUST HOW WE'RE GOING TO DO IT!
?
ALL THE BIG SHOTS WHO COME IN THIS TOWN STAY AT THE RIVERDALE TILTON, AND THAT'S JUST WHERE WE'RE GOING! *COME ON!*
BUT HOW CAN YOU BE SURE HE'LL BE THERE?
2

BECAUSE I'M CERTAIN, ARCH.!
AND WHAT IF HE DOESN'T WANT TO BE DISTURBED AT THE HOTEL?
Archies

RDALE
TON
YOU JUST LEAVE IT TO REGGIE, FELLOWS.! I'LL FIGURE SOME-THING OUT.!
PARK

WILL YOU KINDLY TELL MISTER STARFINDER THAT REGGIE MANTLE, SUPER STAR OF THE ARCHIES, IS HERE TO SEE HIM?
I'M SORRY, BUT WE DON'T HAVE ANY MISTER STARFINDER REGISTERED HERE.!

YOU CAN LEVEL WITH ME, MAC! YOU SEE, HE TOLD ME PERSONALLY HE WAS STAYING HERE.!

YOU MUST BE MISTAKEN, YOUNG MAN.! THERE'S NO SUCH PERSON IN THIS HOTEL.!
OKAY.! HAVE IT YOUR WAY.!
3

WELL, I GUESS HE'S NOT STAYING HERE, REG.!
ARE YOU FOR REAL, ARCH.? THEY ALWAYS SAY THAT WHEN THEY HAVE SOMEBODY LIKE MISTER STARFINDER IN THEIR HOTEL.! IT'S FOR HIS PROTECTION, OTHERWISE HE'D BE PESTERED BY A BUNCH OF TEENAGE KIDS.!
RT
RIVERDALE TILT

I TOOK A QUICK GLANCE AT THE REGISTER! I THINK HE'S IN ROOM 61!
BUT HE WON'T LET US UPSTAIRS.!
LTON

COME ON! WE'RE GOING TO SNEAK IN THE BACK WAY, THROUGH THE HOTEL KITCHEN.!
?

DO YOU THINK WE SHOULD, REGGIE? WHY DON'T WE JUST TAKE OUR CHANCES AT THE T.V. STUDIO.?
DON'T BE SILLY, ARCH.! THIS WAY WE'LL GET A PERSONAL AUDITION.! NOW JUST FOLLOW ME.! I KNOW WHAT I'M DOING.!
KITCHEN DELIVERY ENTRANCE
4

NOW BE QUIET!

?

HEY! JUST WHAT DO YOU THINK YOU'RE DOING?
?
5

PUT THAT FOOD BACK AND COME OVER HERE! YOU DON'T BELONG IN HERE! WHAT ARE YOU KIDS UP TO?
GULP!
OH, NO! THAT BEAN BAG!

COME ON! LET'S GET MOVING!

STOP, YOU KIDS!

WHAT'S GOING ON? WHAT'S ALL THE SHOUTING ABOUT?
THERE WERE A COUPLE OF KIDS IN MY KITCHEN STEALING FOOD! THEY'RE AROUND HERE SOMEWHERE!
6

WHAT ARE YOU TRYING TO DO, JUG, GET US ALL IN TROUBLE? IS THAT ALL YOU EVER THINK OF... FOOD?
I COULDN'T HELP MYSELF! IT SMELLED SO GOOD, I JUST WANTED TO SAMPLE IT!

NOW THEY'LL BE LOOKING FOR US ALL OVER THE HOTEL! YOU MEATHEAD!
WHY DON'T WE JUST FORGET THIS WHOLE IDEA? IT'S FLAKY!

WHAT? AND GIVE UP A CHANCE TO GET INTO SHOW BIZ? NEVER!
OPPORTUNITY COULD BE WAITING FOR US RIGHT AROUND THE CORNER!
AND THAT'S NOT ALL!
39
47-70
7

HERE'S ROOM 61! NOW LET'S BELT OUT A TUNE THAT WILL MAKE HIM JUMP UP AND TAKE NOTICE!
OKAY, BUT I HOPE HE DOESN'T BELT US BACK!
60
61
BAM A DE BAM!
WHAT THE HECK IS GOING ON OUT HERE?
DO YOU LIKE IT, MISTER STARFINDER?
LIKE IT?
8

LET'S SEE HOW YOU LIKE THIS.!
?
BOP!

61
SLAM!
AND THE NAME IS NOT STAR-FINDER.! SO GET OUT OF HERE AND LET ME GET SOME SLEEP.!
63

I KNOW WHAT I DID WRONG, FELLOWS.!
SO DO I.! YOU GOT UP THIS MORNING.!
I'LL BET I LOOKED AT THAT ROOM REGISTER UPSIDE DOWN.! IT WASN'T ROOM 61, IT'S ROOM 19.!
?
9

FORGET IT, REG.! I COULDN'T TAKE ANY-MORE AUDITIONS LIKE THAT.!
COME ON, ARCH.! NOTHING'S GOING TO MAKE ME QUIT.! I'M DETERMINED TO BE DISCOVERED.!

THERE THEY ARE.!

CONSIDER YOURSELF DISCOVERED.!

AND STAY OUT.! IF I CATCH YOU KIDS DISRUPTING MY HOTEL AGAIN, I'LL CALL THE POLICE.!
DELIVERY ENTRANCE
10

WELL, ARE YOU CONVINCED THAT WAS A LOUSY IDEA?

NO! IT WAS JUST OUR BAD LUCK WE DIDN'T GO TO ROOM 19 FIRST! NOW IF I COULD FIGURE OUT ANOTHER WAY!
?

FORGET IT, REG! YOU CAN COUNT US OUT!
THAT'S WHAT'S WRONG WITH YOU GUYS! YOU HAVE NO DRIVE, NO PERSEVERANCE. BUT TAKE ME, I'M DETERMINED TO BE A STAR!
PA

THEN WE SHOULD HAVE GONE OVER TO THE T.V. STUDIO AND TRIED OUR LUCK! NOW IT'S PROBABLY TOO LATE!

WITH A MOB LIKE THEY WOULD HAVE HAD OVER THERE WE WOULDN'T EVEN BE NOTICED!
The Archies
11

SO THERE YOU ARE, ARCHIE.!
I'VE BEEN LOOKING ALL OVER FOR YOU FELLOWS.!

THERE WAS A MISTER STAR-FINDER AT THE HOUSE.! HE WANTED TO TALK TO THE ARCHIES.!
?

IT WAS SOMETHING ABOUT AN AUDITION FOR A MOVIE, BUT HE COULDN'T WAIT ANY LONGER.! HE HAD TO FLY BACK TO THE COAST.!
GULP.!

WHAT ARE YOU FELLOWS DOING?
WE'RE GOING TO USE OUR DRIVE AND PERSEVERANCE AND MAKE REGGIE A SUPER STAR.!
OR A TRACK ONE.!
END

The Archies in "Bubble Trouble"

WHEEEEEEEE
YEA! ARCHIES!
MAN! THE AUDIENCE REALLY FLIPPED OUT!
The Archies

THIS MAGAZINE PUTS US DOWN AS A BUBBLE GUM ROCK GROUP!
HEY, MAN! THAT TEES ME OFF!
The Archi
THE ROCKING ROCK MAGAZINE
RAVING PEBBLE

I WONDER WHAT'S EATING THE BUZZARD WHO WROTE THAT ?
I DON'T KNOW! BUT, I'M GOING TO FIND OUT!
THE ARCHIES TURN US OFF!

ARE YOU THE ONE WHO WROTE THIS ARTICLE ?
WELL! WELL! IF IT ISN'T THE KING OF BUBBLE GUM ROCK HIMSELF!
THE ARCHIES TURN US OFF!
EDITOR

DON'T TAKE IT SO PERSONAL, OLD CHAP!

OUR PUBLICATION HAS HIGH MUSICAL STANDARDS! AND YOUR GROUP DOESN'T MEET THEM!
IS THAT SO ?
2

LOOK! DO YOU KNOW WHO LI'L HARRY IS ?
ROB DILLON
LI'L HARRY
SURE! EVERYONE HAS HEARD OF LI'L HARRY!

BACK IN THE '50S HE WAS ONE OF THE GREAT PIONEERS OF ROCK!

WELL, I SUGGEST YOU GO AND LISTEN TO HIM TONIGHT! YOU MIGHT LEARN SOMETHING!

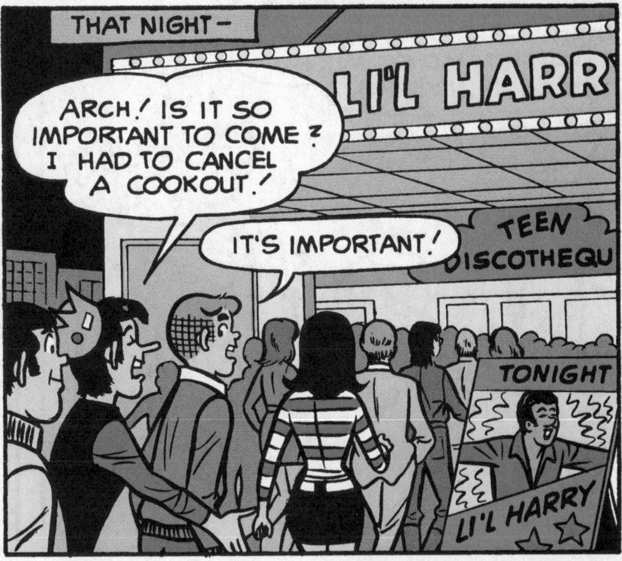
THAT NIGHT—
LI'L HARR
ARCH! IS IT SO IMPORTANT TO COME ? I HAD TO CANCEL A COOKOUT!
IT'S IMPORTANT!
TEEN DISCOTHEQU
TONIGHT
LI'L HARRY

WE'RE GOOD! BUT, WE HAVE TO LEARN IF WE'RE TO CONTINUE TO GROW AS MUSICIANS!
HEY! THAT LI'L HARRY IS SOMETHING ELSE!
YEAH, HE'S FAR OUT!
3

BLESS MY SOOOUL! I THINK I SEE ONE OF MY FAVORITE GROUPS OUT THERE! THE ARCHIES!

COME ON UP AND JOIN ME, ARCHIES!
GEE! WE'VE BEEN HONORED!

WOOH! BAM-A-LAM BAM! I HAVEN'T HAD SO MUCH FUN IN YEARS!
LI'L HARRY

I HOPE THE ARCHIES TOOK MY ADVICE ABOUT COMING HERE!
TONIGH
LI'L HARRY

THEY MIGHT LEARN SOMETHING!
CHIEF! LOOK!

THE ARCHIES!

LI'L HARRY! HOW CAN YOU ALLOW THAT BUBBLE GUM GROUP ON THE SAME STAGE WITH YOU?
4

I DIG 'EM! THAT'S WHY!
BUT THEY PLAY BUBBLE GUM ROCK!

THERE ARE ONLY TWO KINDS OF MUSIC! GOOD MUSIC AND BAD MUSIC!--- ANY MUSIC THAT MAKES PEOPLE HAPPY IS GOOD MUSIC!

PAY NO MIND TO CRITICS! 15 YEARS AGO THEY WERE PUTTING ME DOWN!

BESIDES, I THINK I JUST SET THAT CAT STRAIGHT ABOUT "BUBBLE GUM" MUSIC!
DO YOU THINK SO, LI'L HARRY?

I KNOW SO!
YUK! YUK!
End
5

The Archies in Group Gripe

ARCHIE, OUR INSTRUMENTS ARE GATHERING *DUST!*

YEAH! WE HAVE A BIG DOUBLE GARAGE TO REHEARSE IN BUT WE *DON'T!* HOW COME?

PEOPLE HAVE GOTTEN TIRED OF THE SAME OLD ROUTINES!

The Archies

I CAN'T BELIEVE IT! THE ARCHIES HAVEN'T REHEARSED IN MONTHS!
THEIR DEAFENING DIN USED TO DROWN US OUT!
WE COULDN'T REHEARSE PROPERLY!

SINCE WE'VE HAD THIS QUIET, OUR TRIO HAS MADE *TREMENDOUS PROGRESS!*

I DO BELIEVE WE'RE READY FOR A CONCERT!
YES, BUT WE'LL NEED MONEY FOR PROMOTION AND TO HIRE A HALL!

I'M ONE STEP AHEAD OF BOTH OF YOU! I CLEARED OUT MY ATTIC!
HOW IS THAT GOING TO GET MONEY FOR OUR CONCERT?

OBSERVE!
WEATHERBEE'S
GARAGE SALE
2

I HATE TO DISILLUSION THE OLD BOY, BUT HE WON'T RAISE ENOUGH MONEY TO LIGHT THE SIGN OVER THE CONCERT HALL TICKET WINDOW!
WHO WOULD WANT THIS OLD JUNK OF HIS?
WEATHERBEE'S GARAGE SALE

ARCHIE, WHY DON'T I HEAR YOU REHEARSE ANYMORE?
WE'VE GOTTEN STALE, SIR!

IF WE DON'T FIND A NEW IMAGE, THE ARCHIES ARE FINISHED!
WONDERFUL!

ER---I MEAN--- WHILE YOU'RE SEARCHING FOR THIS "NEW IMAGE," WHY NOT LOOK OVER MY GARAGE SALE?
WHY NOT?
EATHERBEE'S GARAGE SALE

HEY, GUYS! DIG THESE FUNKY TAILS FROM THE THIRTIES!
VRA
WE DO OUR PART
MEMBER
U.S.
3

AND STILL IN AS GOOD SHAPE AS EVER, I MIGHT ADD.!

IF I COULD SAY THE SAME, I'D STILL BE WEARING IT.!

WOZ
DIG ALL THESE BITS OF NOSTALGIA.!
AND THESE FAR-OUT CLOTHES.!

GAD.! THOSE KIDS BOUGHT OUT WEATHERBEE'S ENTIRE STOCK.!
WHICH SAYS MUCH ABOUT THE GULLIBILITY OF TODAY'S YOUTH.!

THERE'S ONE THING YOU CAN SAY ABOUT TODAY'S YOUTH.!
---THEY RECOGNIZE QUALITY.!
4

WE NOW HAVE ENOUGH MONEY TO GO AHEAD WITH OUR CONCERT PLANS!
I'LL BE DARNED!

ALL WE NEED IS ANOTHER MONTH OF GOOD, SOLID REHEARSING!

GOOD HEAVENS! WHAT WAS THAT?

IT SOUNDS LIKE THE ARCHIES HAVE STARTED UP AGAIN!
BUT I THOUGHT THEY WERE THROUGH!

WE *WERE* THROUGH UNTIL THAT GARAGE SALE OF YOURS!
YOUR FUNKY DUDS GAVE US THE *NEW IMAGE* WE WERE SEARCHING FOR!
VRA
MEMBER
U.S.
THE END

CHAPTER THREE

The 1980s

THE ARCHIES IN
SIGN OFF
MAY 1984

SCRIPT: FRANK DOYLE   PENCILS: DAN DECARLO JR.

THE ARCHIES IN
ROCK N' ROLL IS HERE TO SEE
AUGUST 1984

SCRIPT: GEORGE GLADIR   PENCILS: STAN GOLDBERG   INKS: RUDY LAPICK
LETTERS: BILL YOSHIDA   COLORS: BARRY GROSSMAN

SABRINA IN
MONSTER MELODY
DECEMBER 1984

SCRIPT: GEORGE GLADIR   PENCILS: STAN GOLDBERG
LETTERS: BILL YOSHIDA   COLORS: BARRY GROSSMAN

THE ARCHIES IN
THE VOCAL
MAY 1987

SCRIPT: GEORGE GLADIR   PENCILS: STAN GOLDBERG   INKS: RUDY LAPICK
LETTERS: BILL YOSHIDA   COLORS: BARRY GROSSMAN

THE ARCHIES IN
THE NAME OF THE GAME
MARCH 1988

SCRIPT: FRANK DOYLE   PENCILS: DAN DECARLO JR.
INKS: RUDY LAPICK   LETTERS: BILL YOSHIDA

THE Archies in SIGN OFF!

WILL YOU TWO JUVENILES PUT AWAY THAT STUPID FOOTBALL AND HELP LOAD THIS VAN? WE HAVE A GIG TONIGHT!

DO YOU THINK THIS FOOTBALL IS STUPID? I DIDN'T THINK IT WAS STUPID!

WHY, JUST THIS MORNING I WAS DISCUSSING THE METRIC SYSTEM WITH THIS VERY BALL!

ALL RIGHT! ALL RIGHT! DON'T BLOW A GASKET! ONE MORE PASS!

VERY CLASSY ACT, GUYS! WHAT DO YOU DO FOR AN ENCORE?

I KNEW IT! I KNEW IF THERE WAS A WAY TO LOUSE UP OUR GIG, THOSE TURKEYS WOULD THINK OF IT!

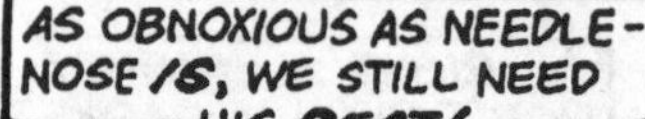
AS OBNOXIOUS AS NEEDLE-NOSE IS, WE STILL NEED HIS BEAT!

RONNIE'S RIGHT! HOW ARE WE GOING TO PLAY A GIG WITHOUT A DRUM?

IF YOU TWO WOULD JUST GROW UP, MAYBE WE COULD MAKE A SUCCESS OUT OF THIS GROUP!

OKAY! OKAY! OKAY! ENOUGH, ALREADY!! STOP WITH THE NAGGING!!

WE'LL TAKE THIS THING AND WE'LL EITHER GET IT REPAIRED OR REPLACED!
BY EIGHT O'CLOCK TONIGHT, AND DON'T FORGET IT!
2

-AND ONE LAST WORD, BEFORE YOU LEAVE--
DON'T TRY TO KID US! WE WEREN'T BORN YESTERDAY!
AR

WITH YOU TWO, THERE'S NO SUCH THING AS A "LAST" WORD!!
ROAR

SHEESH! YOU'D THINK WE STARTED WORLD WAR THREE!!

ONE LITTLE MISTAKE AND THOSE TWO PULL THE PLUG ON YOU!
MAN! YOU'D THINK WE NEVER DID ANYTHING RIGHT!
YEAH!
The ARCHIES

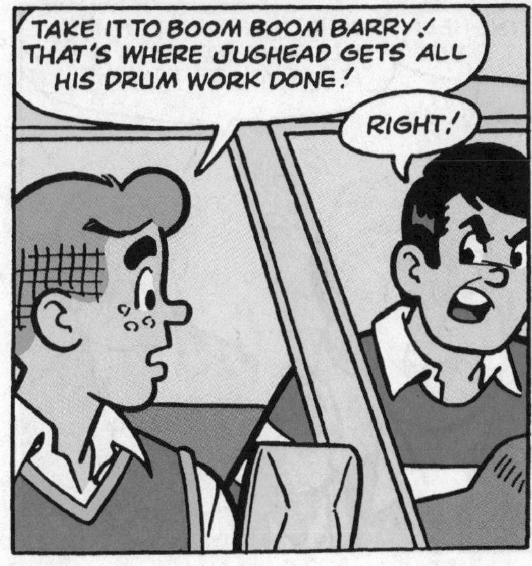
TAKE IT TO BOOM BOOM BARRY! THAT'S WHERE JUGHEAD GETS ALL HIS DRUM WORK DONE!
RIGHT!

WE DID KINDA WRECK IT, DIDN'T WE?
IT WAS JUGHEAD'S FAULT! HE RUINED A MIGHTY FINE PASS!
BOOM BOOM BARRY
DRUMS
3

MY! MY! I THINK THAT DRUMHEAD HAS LOST A BIT OF TENSION!
MAYBE THE MOTHS GOT AT IT!

HEY! WE HAVE A GIG TONIGHT! THIS THING'S GOTTA BE REPAIRED OR RE-PLACED IN A HURRY!
WE'LL HAVE TO GET YOU ONE, I GUESS!

HOW ABOUT THIS? IT'S ABOUT THE SAME MODEL!
GREAT!

ER- JUST ONE THING!
YEAH?

WE GOTTA HAVE THE NAME OF OUR GROUP ON THE DRUMHEAD!

IT'S GONNA COST YOU EXTRA 'CAUSE WE'LL HAVE TO REMOVE THE NAME WHEN YOU RETURN THE DRUM!
FORGET IT! THE NAME'S NOT IMPORTANT!

THE HECK IT'S NOT!
HERE! WRITE OUT WHAT YOU WANT AND WE'LL HAVE IT FOR YOU BY TONIGHT!
4

THEIR DRUMMER SURE HAS A HEAVY HAND WITH THE STICKS!
THAT REDHEAD IS GONNA BE A DOCTOR, I BETCHA!

WHAT MAKES YOU SAY THAT?
'CAUSE HE'LL BE ABLE TO WRITE PRESCRIPTIONS NOBODY CAN UNDER-STAND!

LOOK AT THOSE HENTRACKS, WILL YOU? THERE! THIS IS ABOUT AS CLOSE AS I CAN COME! WHAT DO YOU THINK?
?

WITH THE CRAZY NAMES THEY USE THESE DAYS...THAT MUST BE IT! IT'S THE ONLY WORD I CAN MAKE OUT OF THAT SCRAWL!

WHEN NEW METHODS OF HUMILIATION ARE INVENTED - THOSE TWO WILL BE RESPONSIBLE!
THANKS A HEAP, ARCH!
"THE ANCHOVIES"? NOW THAT'S A FISHY OUTFIT!
YOU REALLY GOT TO WORK ON YOUR HANDWRITING, PAL!
The ANCHOVIES
END.

WOW! SOME OF THESE ROCK ACTS ON NTV ARE *AWESOME*!

ESPECIALLY WHEN THE ACT INCLUDES REGGIE!

THE ARCHIES

THE Archies in "ROCK N' ROLL IS HERE TO ~~STAY~~ SEE"

ON THE OTHER HAND, SOME OF THOSE ROCK ACTS ON TV CAN BE VERY BORING!
TRANSLATED, THAT MEANS REGGIE ISN'T PART OF THEM!
CHIP COOKIES

IT'S 2:15!
AND IN ANOTHER MINUTE IT'LL BE 2:16!

COME ALONG! WE DON'T HAVE A MINUTE TO LOSE!
?

I CHECKED WITH THE NTV PROGRAMMING BEFORE!
AND?
RIVERDALE SHOPPING CENTER

AND THEY'RE ABOUT TO PREVIEW OUR NEW TAPE! WE'RE IN FOR A SUPER TREAT!
AL'S APPLIANCES
?

PRESENTING THE ARCHIES!
HERE WE CAN WATCH OURSELVES SIMULTANEOUSLY ON OVER THIRTY SCREENS!
I DON'T BELIEVE THIS!
SALE $495
2

HATED TO PULL YOU AWAY FROM ALL THOSE TV SCREENS, REG, BUT WE HAVE A REHEARSAL SESSION COMING UP!
WE HAVE TO TAKE CARE OF BUSINESS FIRST!
I'M ONE STEP AHEAD OF YOU!

I HAVE SOMEONE COMING OVER WHO'S GOING TO MAKE OUR GROUP #1!
NO KIDDING!
REHEARSAL STUDIO 1 FLIGHT UP

IS IT A NEW PRODUCER, OR A HOTSHOT SONG-WRITER?
OH, IT'S SOME-ONE BIGGER THAN THAT!

BECAUSE THE VISUAL IS SO IMPORTANT, NOWADAYS A GROUP NEEDS A GREAT HAIRSTYLIST TO MAKE IT ON ROCK VIDEO!
CALL ME 'ZIGGY'!

THIS IS MY CONCEPTION OF HOW THE ARCHIES SHOULD LOOK!
THE Archies

SORRY, ZIGGY! BUT WE'RE HAPPY WITH OUR PRESENT IMAGE!
HMPF! YOU'RE PROBABLY THE ONLY ONES WHO ARE!
STUDIO B
3

REG, SOME OF US DON'T WANT TO CHANGE OUR APPEARANCE!
IT'S OKAY! I FIGURED OUT A WAY AROUND THAT PROBLEM, TOO!

SINCE YOU'RE SO HOMELY-LOOKING WE COULD GET A STAND-IN FOR YOU WHEN WE TAPE A ROCK VIDEO!

DO ME A FAVOR, REG! LET'S FORGET ABOUT ROCK VIDEOS FOR A WHILE!

IN THE MEANTIME, YOU CAN GO GET OUR VAN READY FOR TONIGHT'S GIG!
GOTCHA, EXALTED LEADER!

ONE HOUR LATER...
WHAT'S TAKING REGGIE SO LONG?
I'M GETTING THE VAN READY LIKE YOU TOLD ME!
THE Archies

I'M INSTALLING A VIDEO MACHINE SO WE CAN WATCH OUR TAPES EN ROUTE TO OUR GIGS!
4

HEY! WE'VE REALLY TURNED ON OUR CROWD!
IT'S A PLEASURE TO BE PLAYING AND NOT HAVE TO LISTEN TO REG CARRY ON ABOUT ROCK VIDEOS!
THE Archies

THIS IS A REAL CLASSY PLACE, REG!
I HAVE TO ADMIT YOU DID WELL IN BOOKING US HERE!

THIS PLACE IS BETTER THAN YOU GUYS THINK!
HAVE YOU SEEN THEIR LOUNGE?

THEY HAVE ONE OF THOSE NEW GIANT SCREENS!
NOW WE'LL BE ABLE TO WATCH OURSELVES EVEN DURING OUR BREAKS!
The End

Sabrina (IN) MONSTER MELODY

MY AUNTS HAVE TO BE THE WORLD'S OLDEST FOGIES!
AT 300, THEY HAVE TO BE THE WORLD'S OLDEST ANYTHING!

HMM! SOUNDS LIKE A LIVE GROUP IS REHEARSING IN THAT GARAGE!

HI, NEIGHBORS! MY NAME IS SABRINA!
RIGHT NOW OUR NAME IS 'MUD'!
THE RINK DINK

GEE! YOU BOYS LOOK LOWER THAN A SUNKEN SUBMARINE!
WE FEEL EVEN LOWER!
THE RINKY

NONE OF THE RECORDING OUTFITS WILL LISTEN TO A NEW SONG UNLESS THEY FIRST SEE A VIDEO OF IT!

MAYBE I CAN HELP YOU GUYS!
UH, I JUST HAPPEN TO HAVE A VIDEO CAMERA WITH ME!
ZAP!
2

WHAT GOOD IS A VIDEO CAMERA?
...IT COST AT LEAST $40,000 TO MAKE A DECENT VIDEO!

BESIDES, WHAT'S A CHICK LIKE YOU KNOW ABOUT VISUAL TRICKS AND STUFF LIKE THAT?
YOU'D BE SURPRISED!

FOR EXAMPLE, HOW WOULD YOU GO ABOUT MAKING ME LOOK LIKE A TRIO?

YOU MEAN LIKE THIS!
ZAP!

HOLY COW! THERE ARE THREE OF ME!
HEY! HOW'D YOU DO THAT?
UH, WITH SPECIAL EFFECTS... LIKE IN THE MOVIES!
3

...OR I COULD SUPPLY YOU FELLOWS WITH AN EXOTIC BACKGROUND FOR YOUR VIDEO!

ZAP!
IT'S...IT'S THE EIFFEL TOWER!

HOLY COW! HOW DID YOU GET THE EIFFEL TOWER INTO OUR TINY GARAGE?

LIKE I SAID, YOU CAN DO ALMOST ANYTHING WITH SPECIAL EFFECTS!

I THINK SABRINA KNOWS WHAT SHE'S TALKING ABOUT!
LET HER MAKE OUR VIDEO!

THE ONLY PROBLEM, SABRINA, IS WE WANTED TO MAKE A MONSTER TYPE VIDEO!
--- LIKE MICHAEL JACKSON'S "THRILLER"!

DO YOU KNOW ANYTHING ABOUT MONSTERS AND CREEPY CREATURES?
I THINK I DO!
4

I'D LIKE ALL OF YOU TO STEP INTO THIS CUBBY HOLE ONE AT A TIME... AND CLOSE YOUR EYES!
MAKE UP DEPT.

EEAGH!
DON'T BE FRIGHTENED! IT'S ONLY YOURSELF!

GOSH! SABRINA! YOU'RE FANTASTIC!
ACTUALLY, IT'S JUST A SO-SO JOB! I DON'T HAVE ALL OF MY MAKE-UP EQUIPMENT WITH ME!

IF IT'S NOT ASKING TOO MUCH, SABRINA, COULD YOU THROW IN A FEW SLIMY CREATURES FOR BACKGROUND?

LOOK BEHIND YOU!
5

WHEN THEY SEE THIS VIDEO ON NTV, IT'S GONNA KNOCK 'EM DEAD!
THE RINKY DINKS

LATER:
SABRINA! COME QUICKLY!
?
GOURMET BREW RECIPES

WHAT IS IT, AUNT HILDA?
THERE'S SOMETHING WE WANT TO SHOW YOU!

THIS IS THE KIND OF DECENT SHOW YOU SHOULD BE WATCHING INSTEAD OF THAT TRASH YOU USUALLY HAVE ON!
THE RINKY DINKS
SIGH! ISN'T THAT HAIRY ONE HANDSOME?
END

THE Archies in The VOCAL

ARCHIE, YOUR VOCAL SOUNDS SO GARBLED AND CONFUSING!
WHY DON'T WE DO THE SONG OVER?
DIZZY, DIZZY

WE DON'T HAVE TIME!
BESIDES, THE VOCAL IS UNIMPORTANT! I'M SURE THE OWNER ONLY WANTS TO HEAR WHAT THE BAND SOUNDS LIKE!

FORGET IT, ARCHIE! I'M NOT HIRING ANY BAND THAT MAKES GIBBERISH LIKE THIS!
DIZZY, DIZZY

MIKE, I THINK YOU WERE TOO HARSH ON THAT KID!... HIS SONG HAD A NICE BEAT TO IT!
OH, WHAT DO YOU DEE JAYS KNOW ABOUT THE DISCO BUSINESS?

HE FORGOT HIS DEMO! LET ME HAVE IT! I'LL PLAY IT ON MY SHOW!
HA! HA! BE MY GUEST!

HERE'S A SONG CUT BY THE ARCHIES, A LOCAL GROUP!
LET ME KNOW WHAT YOU THINK OF IT!

I CAN'T UNDERSTAND THE LYRICS!
NEITHER CAN I!

I KNOW! IT'S A SECRET MESSAGE OF SOME SORT!
I BET THE ARCHIES RECORDED THE SONG BACKWARD!

WE'RE GETTING HUNDREDS OF CALLS ASKING US TO DECIPHER THE WORDS OF THAT NEW SONG BY THE ARCHIES!
STATION WLOF

SORRY, BUT I CAN'T HELP YOU!
...IF ANY OF YOU LISTENERS UNDERSTAND THE LYRICS LET ME KNOW!

ONE WEEK LATER:
GREAT NEWS, GUYS! ALL THE LOCAL DEEJAYS ARE PLAYING OUR SONG "DIZZY, DIZZY"!
BUT HOW DID THEY GET OUR DEMO?

WHO CARES?
IN THE PAST WE'VE TRIED SO HARD TO GET A HIT RECORD, AND HERE IT FALLS RIGHT INTO OUR LAPS!
3

MEANWHILE ...
I HAVE ANOTHER ONE OF THOSE ROCK SONGS WITH LYRICS THAT ARE DIFFICULT TO UNDERSTAND!
STATE COMMISSION

IT'S OUR COMMITTEE'S JOB TO GET TO THE BOTTOM OF THIS!
LET'S ASK THE SONG WRITER TO APPEAR BEFORE US!
DIZZY DIZZY

HOLY COW! THE STATE COMMISSION WANTS ME TO APPEAR WITH A COPY OF MY SONG'S LYRICS!
... THEY'RE THINKING OF BANNING MY SONG!

HMM! THE WORDS LOOK INNOCENT ENOUGH! HOW COME THEY SOUND SO GARBLED ON THE TAPE?
I WAS CHEWING GUM AT THE TIME, SIR!

I'VE PLAYED HIS TAPE FORWARD, BACKWARD AND SIDEWAYS!
--- THE LYRICS ARE UNINTELLIGIBLE AT ANY SPEED!
DIRECTORY

I GUESS WE WON'T BE BANNING YOUR SONG AFTER ALL!
THANK YOU, SIR!
4

ARCHIE! BETTY! HAVE YOU HEARD THE LATEST?
WHAT IS IT, JUG?

BECAUSE OUR SONG AROUSED SO MUCH CONTROVERSY, DEEJAYS ALL OVER THE COUNTRY ARE PLAYING IT!
YAHOO! WE'RE #1!
CASHBOX
ARCHIES TOP CHARTS WITH

I GUESS ALL THE FUSS OUR SONG CREATED ONLY MADE PEOPLE WANT TO HEAR OUR RECORD EVEN MORE!
DIZZY DIZZY

GEE! THE ARCHIES ARE OUR IDOLS!
DO YOU HAVE ANY TIPS FOR A GROUP JUST STARTING?
YEAH, I DO!

ALWAYS CHEW GUM WHEN YOU SING!
END

THE Archies
"NAME OF THE GAME"
YOU WANT TO HAVE A *WHAT?*
A P.R. MAN! PUBLIC RELATIONS! HE'LL PUT US ON THE MAP!
THAT'S A FANTASTIC IDEA!
WHO WANTS TO BE ON THE MAP? WE'RE A MUSICAL GROUP, NOT A MAJOR HIGHWAY!
EVERYBODY CAN USE PUBLICITY!
"THE ARCHIES" ARE A HOUSEHOLD WORD!
SO IS "*DIRT*"!

I SAY WE GIVE IT A TRY!

WHERE ARE WE GOING TO FIND A PUBLIC RELATIONS MAN?

I THOUGHT YOU'D NEVER ASK!

FINEST DECISION YOU EVER MADE, FOLKS! IN NO TIME AT ALL YOUR NAME WILL BE ON EVERYBODY'S LIPS!

-BY THE WAY- WHAT IS THE NAME?

"THE ARCHIES"!
NO WONDER NO ONE KNOWS YOU!

FIRST THING WE DO IS GET RID OF THE NAME! THAT'S GOT TO GO!
2

NO WAY! WHAT'S WRONG WITH THE NAME?
LET ME COUNT THE WAYS!

IT'S ALWAYS BEEN A SAPPY NAME!
IT'S BETTER THAN "THE REGGIES"!

I SAY WE LET OUR P.R. MAN HANDLE IT!

HOW ABOUT "BLUE SUGAR"-"DRIVE-TRAIN"-"DEEP SIXES"-"COFFIN NAILS"?
MARVELOUS! I LIKE THEM ALL!

THE PROBLEM IS IN PICKING OUT THE BEST NAME!
I STILL LIKE "THE ARCHIES"!

WHY DON'T WE RUN A TEST?
WHAT KIND OF TEST?

I'LL GET POSTERS MADE USING EACH OF THE FOUR NAMES!
AND?
3

WE SET THEM UP OUT-SIDE WHERE YOU'RE PLAYING – LIKE YOU'RE FOUR DIFFERENT GROUPS!

THEN WE SEE WHICH ONE DRAWS MORE ATTENTION!

THE MAN'S A GENIUS!
IT'S YOUR BALL, PAL-RUN WITH IT!

WE HAVE TO PAY THIS GUY TO THINK UP SILLY NAMES FOR US?
WE OUGHTA CALL OURSELVES "SUCKERS FIVE"!

HEY, WE COULDN'T HAVE HAD A SILLIER NAME THAN "THE ARCHIES"!

THAT NITE:
I'LL SET THESE UP AND WATCH THE REACTIONS OUT HERE!
TONITE

MEANWHILE, WE HAVE TO GO TO WORK! LET'S GO!
TONITE BLUE SUGAR
TONITE DRIVETRAIN
THE DEEP SIX
4

LATER -
WHAT'S GOING ON? WE'VE BEEN PLAYING FOR AN HOUR AND NOBODY'S COME IN!

MAYBE WE'RE LOSING OUR TOUCH!
IT SURE HAPPENED FAST!

WHERE IS EVERY-BODY? LAST NIGHT THE PLACE WAS JUMPING!
ANAGER

I'D BETTER CHECK THE DOOR! MAYBE SOME-BODY FORGOT TO UNLOCK IT!

NO, IT'S NOT THAT! THE DOOR IS OPEN!

WHAT THE HECK ARE THESE THINGS?
UE
AR
TONITE
DRIVETRA

I DON'T HAVE ANY OF THESE GROUPS PLAYING IN MY PLACE!
UE
AR
TONITE
DRIVETRAIN
THE
DEEP
SIX
5

WHO'S THE CREEP WHO'S SABOTAGING MY BUSINESS?
WHAT DO YOU MEAN?

SOMEBODY PUT A BUNCH OF DUMB POSTERS OUTSIDE!
THEY'RE SUPPOSED TO DRAW CUSTOMERS INTO YOUR ESTABLISH-MENT!

WELL, IT'S DRIVING THEM AWAY! THEY TAKE ONE LOOK AND THEY GO ELSEWHERE!

THE ONLY GROUP THEY WANT TO SEE IN HERE IS *THE ARCHIES*!

WELL, SO MUCH FOR PUBLIC RELATIONS!
WELCOME BACK, ARCHIES!!
HOW ABOUT "RIGOR MORTIS"? "ZOMBIEVILLE"? "THE FLATWHEEL FIVE"?
The END

CHAPTER FOUR

The 1990s

THE ARCHIES IN

THE FAME GAME

MARCH 1990

SCRIPT: GEORGE GLADIR   PENCILS: DOUG CRANE
INKS: RICHARD MAURIZIO   LETTERS: ROD OLLERENSHAW

CHUCK CLAYTON IN

WHAT'S IN A NAME?

NOVEMBER 1995

SCRIPT: BILL GOLLIHER   PENCILS: BILL GOLLIHER   INKS: JON D'AGOSTINO
LETTERS: BILL YOSHIDA   COLORS: BARRY GROSSMAN

SABRINA IN

MR. HOAGLAND'S OPUS

NOVEMBER 1997

SCRIPT: BILL GOLLIHER   PENCILS: DAN DECARLO   INKS: DAN DECARLO
LETTERS: BILL YOSHIDA   COLORS: BARRY GROSSMAN

WOW! BEING A SUPERSTAR ISN'T EASY! THERE ARE SO MANY PRESSURES IN THE MUSIC BUSINESS !!
Rolling Pebble

GEE! I WONDER WHAT IT WOULD BE LIKE TO FACE THOSE HEAVY PRESSURES !

ARCHIE!! MEGA RECORDS HAS A FAB CONTRACT FOR YOU!!
BUT THIS CONTRACT HAS ONLY MY NAME ON IT!! IT SAYS NOTHING ABOUT THE OTHER MEMBERS OF MY GROUP!!
THE Archies
The Fame Game
THAT'S BECAUSE WE AT MEGA RECORDS WANT ONLY YOU!!

WE ALL WORKED SO HARD TOGETHER! I CAN'T LEAVE THE GROUP!
BUT, ARCHIE-- IT'S YOUR BIG CHANCE!

FORGET ABOUT US!!
WE CAN'T STAND IN THE WAY OF YOUR SUPER STARDOM!
SIGN THAT CONTRACT, YOU BOZO!

SNIFF! I'LL MISS YOU GUYS!
WE'LL MISS YOU, TOO, ARCHIE!
GATE 7
GATE 7

WHAT A SHOW-STOPPING PERFORMANCE!
WHERE DOES ARCHIE GET ALL HIS ENERGY?
I HEAR HE LOSES TEN POUNDS AT EVERY PERFORMANCE!

WHEW! MY TWENTY-SECOND CONCERT IN ONLY TWENTY-FIVE DAYS! I'M NEAR EXHAUSTION!
YOUR FANS DEMAND ANOTHER ENCORE!

SON, IT'S THREE A.M.! YOU'RE SUPPOSED TO BE RESTING!
MA... I'VE GOT TO FIND TIME TO WRITE MY OWN SONGS IF I WANT TO STAY ON TOP!
2

GOOD NEWS, ARCHIE! FOUR OF YOUR LAST FIVE ALBUMS WENT PLATINUM!!
ONLY FOUR?

I WONDER WHAT WAS WRONG WITH THE FIFTH?! AM I BEGINNING TO SLIP...?

TONIGHT IS "GRAMMY" NIGHT!!
Gosh!! HOW EMBARRASSING IF I DON'T WIN A GRAMMY!!

...AND THIS NEXT GRAMMY GOES TO ARCHIE! ...HIS EIGHTH OF THE YEAR!
WELCOM
AWARD
GRAM

WOE IS ME! EIGHT GRAMMIES!
Gulp! NOW THERE'S TREMENDOUS PRESSURE ON ME TO WIN AGAIN NEXT YEAR, OR I'M A HAS-BEEN!
WHERE WILL I PUT THEM ALL? I DON'T HAVE ANY MORE ROOM ON MY MANTLEPIECE!!
3

IT'S TRUE! I NOW HAVE FAME, MONEY AND GIRLFRIENDS GALORE... BUT AM I REALLY HAPPY?

...AND HOW MUCH LONGER CAN I GO ON BEING THE SAME, SIMPLE ARCHIE, BEFORE SUCCESS TURNS MY HEAD?

EVERYWHERE I GO, MY FANS HOUND ME FOR MY AUTOGRAPH!
Ritzy Arms
POLICE
DO NOT CROSS

I'LL HAVE TO SLIP ON THIS DISGUISE IF I WANT TO GET SOME PEACE!!

LOOK, GIRLS! IT'S HIM! IT'S ARCHIE ANDREWS!

OH, WHY WON'T THEY EVER LEAVE ME ALONE?!
HIS BOWL OF SOUP WILL MAKE A GREAT SOUVENIR!
4

ARCHIE! ARCHIE!!!
POP!
Rolling Pebble

DID YOU SEE THIS ITEM IN TODAY'S PAPER?
NO, BETTY! WHAT DOES IT SAY?

IT SAYS... "A TALENTED YOUNG GROUP CALLED 'THE ARCHIES' PERFORMED LAST NIGHT AT THE TEEN DISCO..."

"...BETTY COOPER SHOWS PLENTY OF PROMISE AS A VOCALIST!"

"...WITH A LITTLE LUCK, SHE MIGHT ONE DAY BECOME A SUPERSTAR!"
SUPER-STAR?!

OH, DEAR BETTY! YOU POOR GIRL! HOW AWFUL!!
?
END

CHUCK! WERE YOU LISTENING TO THE RADIO?!
DID YOU HEAR?! DID YOU HEAR?!
OUCH! I DON'T KNOW IF I'LL EVER BE ABLE TO HEAR AGAIN!
WHAT'S ALL THE YELLING ABOUT?!
CHUCK CLAYTON in WHAT'S IN A NAME?
GUESS WHO I JUST WON A DATE WITH NEXT WEEK?!
A DATE?!
I HAVE NO IDEA!
KING!!
ARF! ARF!

WHO'S THAT?!
KING! MY COUSIN'S DOG! I'M KEEPING HIM WHILE HE'S ON VACATION!

WELL, THAT'S NOT THE KING I WON A DATE WITH! I'M TALKING ABOUT THE ROCK STAR!
WHAT'S WRONG? I'M NOT YOUR TYPE ANYMORE?

DON'T BE RIDICULOUS! IT WON'T BE A REAL DATE! I'LL JUST GO TO HIS CONCERT WITH HIM!

IT'S A CHANCE TO MEET A STAR!
HE'S A STAR, ALL RIGHT! ESPECIALLY IN HIS OWN EYES!

HE DOESN'T EVEN WANT TO BE KNOWN AS KING ANYMORE, DOES HE?!
NO, HE OFFICIALLY CHANGED HIS NAME TO THIS SYMBOL, WHICH HAS NO PRONUNCIATION!

SO NOW EVERYONE CALLS HIM THE ROCK STAR FORMERLY KNOWN AS KING!
HOW STUPID CAN YOU GET!? RIGHT, KING?!
ARF!
2

I THOUGHT MAYBE YOU'D BE EXCITED FOR ME!
IT'S NOT THAT! IT'S JUST I DON'T THINK YOU SHOULD BE HANGIN' WITH THAT GUY!

IF YOU'RE SO WORRIED, YOU CAN FOLLOW US AND KEEP AN EYE ON ME!
THAT'D BE GREAT!
685

THE BIG NIGHT...
CHUCK, I FOUND OUT WE'RE GOING TO THE CONCERT FIRST AND THEN TO DINNER!
OKAY! YOU AND WHAT'S-HIS-SYMBOL, KEEP AN EYE OUT FOR ME!

ARE YOU GOING OUT, SON?!
YEAH! I'LL BE BACK IN A FEW HOURS!

TAKE THIS DOG WITH YOU! I DON'T WANT HIM WANDERING AROUND UNATTENDED!
BUT, MOM, I...

DON'T "BUT, MOM" ME! HE'S YOUR RESPONSIBILITY! YOU TAKE CARE OF HIM!
OKAY!
3

MEANWHILE...
REMEMBER, YOU CAN REFER TO HIM AS KING! BUT WHATEVER YOU DO, DON'T CALL HIM KING!
OKAY!

HERE SHE IS, MISTER... UH... MISTER! YOUR DATE NANCY!
HELLO!

IT'S SO WONDERFUL TO MEET YOU, K... K... CARE FOR SOME GUM ?!
?

YOU KNOW, I REALLY LOVE YOUR MUSIC!
OF COURSE! MOST PEOPLE DO!

SOON...
HERE WE ARE AT THE CONCERT, NANCY! TRY TO BE COOL!
GEE! I'LL TRY MY BEST!

HERE HE IS, JUST IN TIME FOR HIS CONCERT!
NANCY DOESN'T LOOK LIKE SHE'S HAVING MUCH FUN!
ET
4

CAN I HAVE YOUR AUTOGRAPH?!
THERE'S NO TIME! WE HAVE TO GET INSIDE!
HEY!
GRRR!

YO, KING! COME BACK!

ALL RIGHT! WHO SAID THAT?!
I DID! BUT I WAS...

I DON'T WANT TO BE CALLED THAT ANYMORE! YOU GOT IT?!
SURE, MAN!
?

MEET MY FRIEND KING --HE'S VERY PROTECTIVE!
UH-OH!
GRRR!

HEY, MAN! CALL OFF YOUR DOG!
I WOULD IF I COULD, BUT WOULDN'T YOU KNOW, HE CHANGED HIS NAME TO SOMETHING I CAN'T PRONOUNCE!
The END

Sabrina in MR. HOAGLAND'S OPUS?

HI, GINA!
HI, BRIAN! SEE YOU IN THE BAND!
GINA! WHERE'VE YOU BEEN HIDING ***HIM?*** HAVEN'T SEEN HIM AROUND!

YOU'LL NEVER BE ABLE TO OUTPLAY BRIAN!
YES! BUT MAYBE WE CAN MAKE BEAUTIFUL MUSIC TOGETHER!

LATER:
SO, SABRINA, YOU SAY YOU WANT TO TRY OUT FOR THE BAND! WHAT DO YOU PLAY?
THE SAXOPHONE!

WHY DON'T YOU COME TO THE BAND PRACTICE TOMORROW AND TRY OUT?
SOUNDS GREAT, MR. HOAGLAND!

THE NEXT MORNING...
SO YOU'RE TRYING OUT FOR THE BAND TODAY! CAN I HEAR YOU?
I'M A LITTLE RUSTY... BUT, OKAY!

OH, BROTHER... SHE'S HORRIBLE! I'LL HAVE TO FIND A WAY TO LET HER DOWN EASY THIS AFTERNOON!

GOOD LUCK, SABRINA! YOU'RE GOING TO NEED IT!
THAT WAS BAD! I'M GOING TO USE MY POWERS TO IMPROVE MY PLAYING!
2

MUSIC THAT SOOTHES THE SAVAGE BEAST, GIVE YOUR GIFT TO ME SO I CAN'T BE BEAT!

THAT AFTERNOON...
HI, SABRINA! I'VE BEEN EXPECTING YOU!
THANKS, MR. HOAGLAND!

WATCH OUT OVER THERE!
BONK!

SABRINA... ARE YOU OKAY?
I'M FINE! JUST A LITTLE DAZED!

IF YOU DON'T WANT TO TRY OUT NOW, I'LL UNDERSTAND!
NO, I WANT TO! HERE GOES!

SABRINA, THAT'S REMARKABLE!
3

WHAT HAPPENED ?! I OVERHEARD YOU THIS MORNING AND YOU WERE HORRIBLE!
YOU DID ?!

OF COURSE! IT MUST'VE BEEN THE KNOCK ON THE HEAD! I'VE READ ABOUT THOSE THINGS!
OH, YEAH ?!

CLASS, MEET SABRINA! OUR NEW FIRST-SEAT SAXOPHONIST!
AN ACCIDENT HAS TURNED HER INTO A VIRTUOSO!
HUH ?

EXCUSE ME BRIAN, BUT THIS IS NOW SABRINA'S SEAT!
SORRY, NICE TO MEET YOU!
HMPH!

NOW, LET'S HEAR OUR NEW NUMBER FROM THE TOP!

STOP IT! THAT'S HORRIBLE, PEOPLE!
4

EXCEPT FOR YOU, OF COURSE, SABRINA!
THANKS!

MAYBE YOU SHOULD GO SOLO! WHY DON'T YOU STAY LATE AND WE'LL PRACTICE!
BUT I JUST WANTED TO BE IN THE BAND!

NONSENSE! WE CAN'T DEPRIVE THE WORLD OF YOUR TALENT! YOU'LL BE MY PROTEGE!
BUT WE MUST PRACTICE! PRACTICE! PRACTICE!
HOO, BOY!

THIS ISN'T AT ALL WHAT I HAD IN MIND! BRIAN'S EVEN MAD AT ME! THERE'S ONLY ONE WAY OUT OF THIS!!
ZAP!

CRASH!
BONK!
SABRINA! ARE YOU OKAY?

FINE! LET'S PRACTICE!
5

WHAT HAPPENED ?

IT MUST'VE BEEN THIS SECOND KNOCK ON THE HEAD! I SEEM TO HAVE LOST MY ABILITY!
OH, NO!

MY DISCOVERY IS GONE! MY DREAMS SHATTERED!
DON'T TAKE IT TOO HARD, SABRINA! I CAN ALWAYS HELP YOU LEARN AGAIN!
THANKS, BRIAN!

LATER...
THAT WAS THE WEIRDEST THING! GETTING AND LOSING YOUR TALENT BY GETTING BONKED WITH A BASKET-BALL!
WHAT CAN I SAY, GINA? LIFE IS STRANGE!

I JUST HOPE HOAGLAND BEGINS TO HANDLE IT A LITTLE BETTER!
I KNOW WHAT YOU MEAN!
The End

CHAPTER FIVE

The 2000s

JOSIE IN

OH SOLO MIO

DECEMBER 2001

SCRIPT: DAN PARENT PENCILS: HOLLY G! INKS: JOHN COSTANZA
LETTERS: BILL YOSHIDA COLORS: BARRY GROSSMAN

SABRINA IN

BETWEEN A ROCK AND A HARD PLACE

MARCH 2003

SCRIPT & PENCILS: HOLLY G! INKS: AL NICKERSON

THE ARCHIES IN

BATTLE OF THE BANDS - PART 1

DECEMBER 2008

SCRIPT: JANE SMITH FISHER PENCILS: STAN GOLDBERG INKS: BOB SMITH
LETTERS: JACK MORELLI COLORS: GLENN WHITMORE

THE ARCHIES IN

BATTLE OF THE BANDS - PART 2

JANUARY 2009

SCRIPT: JANE SMITH FISHER PENCILS: STAN GOLDBERG INKS: RICH KOSLOWSKI
LETTERS: JACK MORELLI COLORS: GLENN WHITMORE

THE ARCHIES IN

THE ARCHIES IN NEW YORK

OCTOBER 2009

SCRIPT: HAL LIFSON PENCILS: DAN PARENT INKS: RICH KOSLOWSKI
LETTERS: JACK MORELLI COLORS: GLENN WHITMORE

Josie and the Pussycats in "Oh Solo Mio"

PART ONE

OUR NEW SINGLE IS GOING TO BE A SMASH!

THAT WAS A *GREAT* SESSION, GIRLS!

NO! NO! NO! THIS CAN'T HAPPEN TO ME!
ARE YOU OKAY?
STUDIO B

NO... MY RECORDING ARTIST WAS A NO SHOW!! I HAVE TO RECORD A SOFT DRINK JINGLE!
DO YOU KNOW ANY SINGERS?

WELL, I MIGHT! AFTER ALL, I'M JOSIE...
OF "JOSIE AND THE PUSSYCATS"? I LOVE YOUR MUSIC!

ANY INTEREST IN MAKING SOME EXTRA MONEY?
WELL, I NEVER DID A JINGLE!

IT PAYS ...PSSSST... PSSSST...
ZOWIE!!

THAT'S MORE THAN I MAKE IN A YEAR!!
I GUESS I COULD HELP YOU OUT A BIT!
2

A LOT OF CELEBRITIES DO COMMERCIALS!
SO...
SCHLEPSI COLA'S SIMPLY COOL, DRINK NO OTHER, DON'T BE A FOOL...
GREAT!!
JOSIE! YOU'VE SAVED THE DAY!
NO PROBLEM!
SOON...
JOSIE!! WHAT'S THIS I HEAR ABOUT YOU DOING A SCHLEPSI JINGLE?
IT WAS A SPUR OF THE MOMENT THING! WHY?
ROCK STAR
CHIPS
WHY?! I'M YOUR AGENT! EVERYTHING GOES THROUGH ME!
WRONG-O! "JOSIE AND THE PUSSYCATS" GOES THROUGH YOU!! THIS WAS SOLO WORK!
ROCK STAR
SO... YOU'RE GOING SOLO?
NO! IT WAS JUST A FLUKE THING!
ROCK STAR
3

HONESTLY! SOME PEOPLE LIKE TO MAKE MOUNTAINS OUT OF MOLE HILLS!

HEY, GIRLS! READY TO... UH-OH! I DON'T LIKE THOSE ICY LOOKS!
WHEN WERE YOU GOING TO TELL US YOU'RE BREAKING UP THE BAND?

IT WAS ONE LOUSY JINGLE! HOW'D YOU FIND OUT SO QUICKLY?
I THOUGHT THESE POOR GIRLS NEEDED TO FIND OUT THE TRUTH FROM A TRUSTED FRIEND!
SO, WHY'D YOU TELL THEM?
VERY FUNNY! CALL ME WHEN YOU NEED A REPLACEMENT!

SOON...
NOW THAT I'VE EXPLAINED EVERYTHING, LET'S JAM!
WE STILL NEED TO REWORK THE CHORUS ON OUR NEW SONG, FIRST!

I THINK THE OLD CHORUS WORKS FINE!
IT NEEDS MORE! THIS ISN'T A SOFT DRINK JINGLE, YOU KNOW!
4

THAT'S IT!! I'M TAKING A BREAK!
FINE! MAYBE WE SHOULD ALL TAKE A BREAK!
BINK 281

SOUNDS GOOD TO ME!!
THIS ISN'T JUST A COFFEE BREAK IS IT?
SLAM!

SOON
JOSIE! THE COMPANY LOVES YOUR JINGLE SO MUCH, THEY WANT YOU TO APPEAR IN THE COMMERCIAL!
SOUNDS GOOD! I'M TAKING A BREAK FROM THE PUSSYCATS ANYWAYS!

GOOD! I'M HARLAN, FROM THE SCHLEPSI CORPORATION! I'LL BE YOUR NEW "SOLO" AGENT!!
OH, I ALREADY HAVE ONE!

YES, BUT I'LL REPRESENT YOUR SOLO VENTURES! YOU ARE TRYING TO ESTABLISH A "SOLO" CAREER AREN'T YOU?
ER-WELL I GUESS MAYBE I AM!

NOW, WE NEED SOME NEW JINGLES FOR SCHLEPSI!
SURE, SONG-WRITING IS MY FORTE!
5

LATER...
SHEESH! I CAN'T COME UP WITH A SINGLE JINGLE!
IT'S A LOT EASIER TO WRITE WHEN YOU CAN BOUNCE IT OFF TWO OTHER HEADS!
DAY DREAM

SO...
JOSIE! HOW'S IT GOING?
TERRIBLE!! I CAN'T COME UP WITH A SINGLE THING!!
BEEP

NO PROBLEM! HERE'S SOME JINGLES OUR AD AGENCY CAME UP WITH!
AD AGENCY?

YOUR VOICE AND LOOK ARE THE MOST IMPORTANT THING ANYWAY!
MEET CLAIRE, YOUR STYLIST!

WHAT'S WRONG WITH MY LOOK?
NOTHING! BUT THIS IS THE "NEW" SOLO YOU! OUT WITH THE OLD, IN WITH THE NEW!

YEAH, OUT WITH THE OLD...
Josie
AND THE
PUSSYCATS
CONTINUED 6

JOSIE AND THE PUSSYCATS in "OH SOLO MIO" PART TWO

THAT'S OUR JOSIE?!
SHE LOOKS LIKE A MANNEQUIN! IT'S NOT HER!
AND THE MUSIC IS SO GENERIC!! IT SOUNDS SO POLISHED!!
Josie for SCHLEPSI Cola

I...ER... READ IT IN A TRADE PAPER! I MUST'VE MISPLACED IT!
I THINK IT'S TIME TO LOOK FOR A NEW LEAD PUSSYCAT!

I HATE TO ADMIT IT, BUT SHE MAY BE RIGHT!
IT LOOKS LIKE JOSIE'S SPLIT! TIME TO LOOK FOR A NEW PUSSYCAT!

I HAVE SOMEONE PERFECT IN MIND!
ALEXANDRA & the PUSSYCATS!!!
WINK
SO...
JOSIE, YOU'RE SO POPULAR! WE'RE MAKING YOU THE NEW SCHLEPSI GIRL!
I'M SO POPULAR AND SO MISERABLE!!

WHAT!? HOW CAN YOU FEEL THIS WAY?
I'M AN ARTIST, NOT A PAINTED FASHION DOLL TO SELL SOFT DRINKS!

IT'S BEEN FUN, BUT IT'S BACK TO ROCK 'N' ROLL FOR ME!
BUT THERE'S TONS OF MONEY TO BE MADE!
8

THERE'S NOT ENOUGH MONEY IN THE WORLD TO SELL MY SOUL! GOOD-BYE!
WHAT PLANET IS SHE FROM?

LATER...
JOSIE? WHERE ARE YOU GOING?
I'M GOING TO REGROUP WITH MELODY AND VAL!
RAD RECORDING STUDIO

DIDN'T YOU HEAR? THEY'RE LOOKING FOR A NEW LEAD SINGER!
WHAT?! ARE YOU MAKING THIS UP?!

TAKE A LOOK!
I GUESS I'VE BLOWN IT! SOB-WISH THEM LUCK FOR ME!
PUSSYCAT TRYOUTS
TODAY 1-3PM

SO...
JOSIE! ARE YOU ALL RIGHT?
I'M BEING REPLACED! HOW AM I SUPPOSED TO FEEL?

BUT ALEXANDRA SAID YOU WERE GOING TO RECORD A SOLO CD!
WHERE'D SHE HEAR THAT?
9

SHE SAID SHE READ IT IN A TRADE PAPER!
AND YOU BELIEVED HER?

WELL, YOU ARE GETTING VERY POPULAR!
YEAH, ONLY AS A "BARBIE DOLL", NOT AN ARTIST!
IT'S NOT THE SAME! I WANTED TO RETURN, BUT MAYBE IT'S ALL TOO LATE!

SOON AT ALEX'S PLACE...
BEFORE YOU SAY MORE, LOOK AT THIS CONCERT FOOTAGE I'M PUTTING TOGETHER!
OUR LAST TOUR!
CLICK!

JUST LOOK AT US TOGETHER!! YOU CAN'T BUY THE CHEMISTRY WE HAVE TOGETHER!
THANK YOU, DETROIT!

THE THREE OF YOU ARE MAGIC! YOU CAN'T MESS WITH THAT!
THANKS FOR SHOWING ME THAT CLIP! LET'S GO VISIT A COUPLE OF PUSSY-CATS!

AT THE TRYOUTS...
NEXT PLEASE!
WHY ARE THEY ALL SO BAD, VAL?
PUSSYCAT
TRY-OUTS
10

LET'S FACE IT! "JOSIE AND THE PUSSYCATS" WORK BECAUSE OF "JOSIE AND THE PUSSYCATS"!
NOBODY ELSE HAS THAT SPECIAL SOMETHING...

...UNTIL NOW!
ALEXANDRA! DON'T EVEN TRY TO...

GIVE ME YOUR HEART...
...SING!!!

GET OUT!
YEAH! TRYOUTS ARE OVER!
AW, C'MON! JUST ONE MORE! PUH-LEASE!

I HEARD YOU'RE LOOKING FOR A NEW SINGER!!
YOU'VE GOT THE JOB!
WOW! YOU LOOK JUST LIKE OUR OLD SINGER!
MELODY! THIS IS JOSIE!!
WHEW! I THOUGHT YOU WERE AN EVIL TWIN OR SOMETHING!
IT'S GOOD TO BE BACK!
END

Sabrina
"Between A Rock And A Hard Place!"
TALENT CONTEST
Sat.
Come One Come All
FUN FUN
TeenTour
FRENCH CLUB
CATS
CDs 4 Sale
Babysitting
Amy
TSK YOU'D THINK AMY WAS, LIKE, SHAKEARA OR SOMETHING!
I'M SOOO SICK OF HER SHOWING OFF ABOUT HER DANCE NUMBER FOR THE TALENT SHOW!
REALLY? I'D THINK YOU'D BE SICK OF AMY FLIRTING WITH HARVEY!
GRRR
THAT'S IT! AMY HAS TO BE STOPPED!
1

HOW?
I'LL THINK OF SOMETHING!
ZAP
BURP!

HEY, HARVEY, WHAT'S UP?
HEY, SABRINA!
EXCUSE ME...

...I WAS JUST TELLING HARVEY ABOUT MY FABULOUS OUTFIT FOR MY DANCE ROUTINE...TILL YOU INTERRUPTED!

OH, YEAH-UM-MY OUTFIT IS WAY COOL, TOO!
YOU'RE GONNA DANCE IN THE TALENT SHOW? I'VE SEEN YOU DANCE...

...YOU'RE ABOUT AS GRACEFUL AS A BLINDFOLDED PENGUIN!
YEAH? WELL, I'VE GOT A BAND! ...A ROCK BAND!

COOL, SABRINA! I DIDN'T KNOW YOU HAD A BAND!
YEAH--SURE! WHY NOT?
2

FINE, WE'LL SEE HOW YOUR LITTLE ROCK BAND DOES AGAINST MY SUPERIOR DANCE SKILLS!
WOW! I'M DATING A ROCK STAR! CAN'T WAIT TO SEE YOU JAM! LATER, BABE, I'M LATE FOR HISTORY!
THAT'S RIGHT, HARV! I'M A REGULAR JOSIE AND THE PUSSYCATS!
LATER THAT EVENING...
YOU TOLD THEM WHAT?!
THAT I HAD A ROCK BAND! JULIE, PLEASE TELL ME YOU PLAY GUITAR OR SOMETHING!
THE TALENT SHOW IS THIS WEEKEND!
I CAN BEEP OUT 'HAPPY BIRTHDAY' ON MY POCKET CALCULATOR! THAT'S THE EXTENT OF MY SUPER-STAR TALENT!
SORRY I CAN'T BE ANY HELP, SABRINA!
THANKS ANYWAY, JULIE! SIGH I'LL FIGURE SOMETHING OUT!
3

DARN! WHY DID I SAY SUCH A STUPID THING ?!!
BAM
?
PLOP
CINDERELLA! Humm-- THAT GIVES ME AN IDEA!
Cinderella
WHEN CINDI NEEDED COACH-MEN, HER FAIRY GODMOTHER JUST ZAPPED A BUNCH OF MICE!
ZAP!
POOF
I'LL JUST ZAP UP MY BAND! HURRAY! ALL I HAVE TO DO IS PICK OUT MY OUTFIT!
THAT WEEKEND...
SABRINA, YOU'RE ON NEXT!
EXCELLENT! NOW TO ZAP THESE ROCKS INTO ROCKERS USING THE 'CINDERELLA SPELL'!
ZAP
4

LADIES AND GENTLEMEN... SABRINA SPELLMAN AND HER BAND... 'ROCKPILE'!
WHOA!
COOL!
WOW! LOOK AT THOSE COSTUMES!
I WANNA ROCK!
HALF-HOUR LATER...
GRRRR
MORE! MORE! MORE!
Amy
OKAY, BOYS, THEY WANT MORE, SO LET'S ROCK ON!
11:59 p.m. AND SIX ENCORES LATER...
12:00 a.m.
EEP!
Poof
Poof
Poof
5

?!
YAHOO!
YAH!

...AND FIRST PRIZE GOES TO... SABRINA SPELLMAN!

1ST

THAT WAS AN *INCREDIBLE* STAGE SHOW! COMPUTER GENERATED, RIGHT? HIDDEN PROJECTORS, RIGHT?

1ST

ER--THAT'S *RIGHT*! IT'S JUST AMAZING THE *MAGIC* YOU CAN MAKE WITH COMPUTERS THESE DAYS!

1ST

END

6

IT'S TIME FOR RIVERDALE HIGH'S BATTLE OF THE BANDS, SPONSORED BY THE RIVERDALE MUSIC EMPORIUM...
... FIRST PRIZE IS AN ALL EXPENSES PAID TRIP TO A TROPICAL ISLAND!
Archie & FRIENDS
IN
BATTLE OF THE BANDS
PART ONE
SUN
JUGHEAD! WHERE'S THE FIRE?!
THE KITCHEN! IT'S LUNCH-TIME!
WELL, IT'LL HAVE TO WAIT! I'VE GOT BIG NEWS!
TELL EVERYONE TO MEET ME AT POP'S AFTER SCHOOL!
1

ARCHIE, WHAT'S SO IMPORTANT?
THIS BETTER BE IMPORTANT! I'VE GOT PLACES TO BE AND PEOPLE TO MEET!

I'M SURE YOU ALL HEARD ABOUT THE BATTLE OF THE BANDS AT SCHOOL! THE ARCHIES CAN SNAP UP THAT PRIZE NO PROBLEM! LIKE TAKING CANDY FROM A BABY!
I KNOW, ARCHIE... BUT-- THE LAST TIME THE ARCHIES PLAYED TOGETHER WE GOT INTO A TERRIBLE FIGHT! REMEMBER, WE ALMOST DIDN'T PLAY AT ALL!
CHOMP! MUNCH!

SORRY, ARCHIEKINS, BUT I DON'T KNOW IF THE ARCHIES SHOULD EVER PLAY AGAIN!
WELL, THAT'S SETTLED! NOW IF YOU'LL EXCUSE ME-- I'VE GOT MY OWN NEWS--A HOT DATE!

DID YOU HEAR THE TOP PRIZE IS A TROPICAL ISLAND VACATION?!
2

REALLY?! A TRIP FOR ALL OF US?!
NOW YOU'RE TALKING! COUNT ME IN!

I'M STILL NOT SURE ABOUT THIS! I THINK WE HAD BAD MUSICAL KARMA!
COME ON, JUGGIE! WHAT COULD GO WRONG? THINK OF ALL THOSE TROPICAL MILK SHAKES!

ACTUALLY, IT MIGHT NOT BE THAT EASY TO WIN! I'VE HEARD SOME OF THOSE BANDS, AND THEY'RE REALLY GOOD!
DILTON, MAYBE YOU SHOULD STICK TO THE BOOKS AND LEAVE THE MUSIC TO US!
POPS MENU

YEAH!
I'M IN!
LET'S DO THIS THING!!
I HOPE THIS WORKS!
3

A FEW DAYS LATER, REGGIE MEETS THE ENEMY...
HEY, AREN'T YOU REGGIE? YOU PLAY WITH THE ARCHIES!
THAT'S RIGHT, SUGAR!
I'VE HEARD YOU PLAY. THAT'S ONE HOT BAND. AND YOU'RE ONE HOT GUY!
I'M TINA! I PLAY IN A BAND, TOO!
REALLY? WHICH ONE?
IT'S AN ALTERNATIVE BAND. THE STOPS AND STARTS.
WAIT A MINUTE! THAT BAND IS COMPETING IN THE BATTLE OF THE BANDS! I DON'T THINK THIS IS A GREAT TIME TO GET TO KNOW EACH OTHER!
TOO BAD! I THINK WE COULD MAKE SOME GREAT MUSIC TOGETHER!
HERE'S MY NUMBER IN CASE YOU CHANGE YOUR MIND!
4

MAN! ARCHIE WOULD KILL ME IF HE SAW ME WITH A GIRL FROM ANOTHER BAND!

'COURSE, WHAT ARCHIE DOESN'T KNOW CAN'T UPSET HIM!

HOPE YOU DON'T MIND THIS OUT OF THE WAY PLACE! I HATE GOING TO THE SAME SPOTS WHERE EVERYONE KNOWS EACH OTHER!
NO PROBLEM! I'M HAPPY YOU CALLED ME!

SO, HAS YOUR BAND BEEN PRACTIC-ING FOR THE CONTEST?
NOT YET! WE'LL PROBABLY START SOON! WE COULD USE SOME PRACTICE!

WE NEED LOTS MORE PRACTICE! I'M NOT SURE WE'LL EVER BE READY! AND I REALLY WANT TO WIN THAT TRIP! I'VE NEVER BEEN ON A PLANE BEFORE!

IT SOUNDS LIKE TINA NEEDS THAT TRIP MORE THAN I DO! MAYBE THE ARCHIES DON'T HAVE TO WIN THAT CONTEST AFTER ALL!
5

MEANWHILE, DILTON HAS HIS WORK CUT OUT FOR HIM...
ARCHIE DIDN'T BELIEVE ME ABOUT THE OTHER BANDS, AND NOW IT'S UP TO US TO CONVINCE HIM!
US?!

YES. US. AS IN YOU AND ME. YOU WANT TO WIN THAT PRIZE, DON'T YOU?
I GUESS SO. I STILL DON'T THINK IT'S GOING TO HAPPEN.

TRUST ME. ONCE ARCHIE FACES HIS COMPETITION, YOU'LL HAVE A BETTER CHANCE OF WINNING THIS COMPETITION!
JUST COME WITH ME!

I SCOPED OUT THE REHEARSAL SIGHTS FOR THE OTHER BANDS! WITH MY DIGITAL RECORDER, WE'LL DELIVER ALL THE PROOF ARCHIE NEEDS!

YOU WERE RIGHT, DILT! THIS BAND IS GREAT!
WAIT'LL YOU HEAR THE OTHERS! WE JUST CAN'T GET CAUGHT DOING THIS! WE HAVE TO BE VERY CREATIVE IN OUR APPROACH!
6

ROCK ROCKERS
SUPER S
7

WHERE HAVE YOU TWO BEEN?
NEVER MIND WHERE WE'VE BEEN... WAIT'LL YOU HEAR WHAT WE HEARD!

WE TAPED YOUR COMPETITION FOR THE COMPETITION. LISTEN TO THIS!

MAN! DILTON, YOU WERE RIGHT!
THEY SOUND GREAT!

NOW LISTEN TO THE OTHERS!
I CAN'T BELIEVE THIS! ALL OF THEM SOUND GREAT!

I'VE GOT TO GET EVERY-BODY OVER HERE! WE'VE GOT SOME SERIOUS REHEARSING TO DO!
8

WE'D BETTER PLAY BETTER THAN EVER IF WE'RE GOING TO WIN THIS THING!

LET'S GET STARTED!

The Archies

ONE, TWO... ONE, TWO, THREE...

TELL IT TO ME BABY!

TELL ME WHAT YOU'RE SAYING!

STOP! STOP!!

LOOKS LIKE REGGIE CAN'T STAY AWAY FROM THE FORBIDDEN FRUIT...
I'M HAPPY TO SEE YOU AGAIN, REGGIE! WHERE IS THIS MYSTERY PLACE YOU'RE TAKING ME TO ?!

I THOUGHT WE SHOULD GET OUT OF RIVERDALE. YOU KNOW, AWAY FROM THE CROWDS!
I KNOW WHAT YOU MEAN. YOU CAN'T GO ANYWHERE WITH-OUT SEEING SOME-ONE YOU KNOW!
EAST CENTRAL PARK

HOW'S YOUR BAND DOING? ARE YOU READY FOR THE CONTEST?
WE'RE GETTING THERE... BUT WE ONLY HAVE A WEEK BEFORE THE CONCERT!

HOW 'BOUT THE ARCHIES? ARE YOU READY?

WE'RE HAVING SOME... PROBLEMS. GEE... I JUST CAN'T GET MY ACT TOGETHER. YOU MIGHT HAVE A BETTER CHANCE THAN YOU THINK!
10

MEANWHILE, BETTY AND VERONICA HAVE THEIR OWN PRIORITIES FOR THE CONTEST...
RON, LOOK AT THIS!
C'MON, GUYS! LET'S SEE HOW YOU LOOK!
YOUNG MEN'S FASHIONS

UH... NOT TOO SURE ABOUT THIS, GIRLS!
OH, NO! WHAT WAS I THINKING?

HERE! TRY THESE!

NEXT! NOT THAT!
DEFINITELY NOT THAT!
ROCK ROLL
11

THAT'S BETTER! YOU LOOK SO COOL. WE COULD WIN ON OUR LOOKS ALONE!
YEAH, YOU LOOK GREAT! OH, WAIT... MY PHONE IS RINGING!
BEEDLE BOOP

HI, DADDYKINS!
REALLY?!
WOW! EXCELLENT! BYE, DADDY!
DADDY HAS GREAT NEWS! THE FORECAST CALLS FOR FRESH SNOW IN COLORADO! AND SINCE WE'RE OFF FROM SCHOOL FOR STAFF DEVELOPMENT, WE'RE GOING SKIING!
SKIING!? WHAT ABOUT REHEARSAL?!

DON'T WORRY, ARCHIEKINS! YOU'LL FIND SOMEONE TO FILL IN FOR ME! ANYWAY, I'LL BE BACK FOR AT LEAST ONE REHEARSAL ON FRIDAY!
WE'LL BE FINE!
YOUNG MEN'S FASHIONS
12

A FEW DAYS LATER...
WELL, THAT WAS MY LAST SHOT! I CAN'T FIND ANYONE TO REHEARSE WHILE RON IS AWAY!
MILK

I'M BEGINNING TO THINK YOU WERE RIGHT ABOUT OUR BAD MUSICAL KARMA, JUG!
COLA

MAYBE I CAN HELP!
THANKS, DILTON, BUT THERE AREN'T ANY MATH FORMULAS OR GADGETS THAT CAN GET US OUT OF THIS MESS!
MILK

I TOOK A FEW YEARS OF PIANO LESSONS. MAYBE I COULD TRY OUT THE KEYBOARD!
HE'S OUR LAST CHANCE, ARCHIE!

I GUESS I DON'T HAVE A CHOICE. MEET US FOR REHEARSAL TOMORROW!
13

COUNT-DOWN... THREE DAYS 'TIL THE SHOW...
I HOPE YOU'RE READY, DILTON. LET'S TAKE IT FROM THE TOP! HIT IT!
STOP!
RIIINGG!
I WAS AFRAID OF THIS, DILTON. YOU'VE GOT TO STEP UP THE PACE! AND REGGIE! -- YOUR SOLO'S STILL NOT RIGHT! WHAT'S WRONG?!
HI, RON! HOW'S THE SKIING?
I DON'T KNOW... I'M JUST NOT FEELING IT! DON'T WORRY, WE STILL HAVE A FEW DAYS. I'LL GET THERE!
VERONICA! HURRY BACK!
REALLY? ARE YOU SURE?
OK! I'LL TELL ARCHIE!
14

UH... ARCH...
MY HEAD'S NOT IN A GREAT PLACE RIGHT NOW, BETTY. I HOPE IT'S GOOD NEWS.

WELL, IT'S ABOUT VERONICA.
THAT WAS HER ON THE PHONE, RIGHT? PLEASE TELL ME SHE'S COMING HOME EARLY!

NOT EXACTLY...
THEN WHAT DID SHE SAY? SHE'LL BE HOME FRIDAY, WON'T SHE?
NOT SURE.

THE FORECAST IS REALLY BAD FOR FRIDAY! RON DOESN'T THINK SHE CAN GET OUT UNTIL IT STOPS SNOWING!
WHAT?! WE CAN'T WIN WITH-OUT VERONICA!

DON'T SAY THAT, ARCHIE! WE STILL HAVE A CHANCE! DILTON WILL DO NOTHING BUT PRACTICE UNTIL SATURDAY!
AND REGGIE WILL GET HIS ACT TOGETHER. I REALLY WANT TO WIN THIS TRIP!
I WON'T LET YOU DOWN, ARCHIE!
HEY, DOES THIS MEAN I CAN GO ON THE TRIP?!
THERE WON'T BE A TRIP. WE'LL NEVER WIN. BUT IF YOU WANT THIS SO BADLY, I GUESS WE CAN STILL TRY.
15

TWO DAYS BEFORE THE CONTEST, AND THE PLOT IS ABOUT TO THICKEN...

I KNOW YOUR BAND WILL BE HERE ANY MINUTE. I JUST WANTED TO ASK IF I COULD SEE YOU TONIGHT!
YEAH, THAT WOULD BE GREAT. SEE YOU LATER.

I CAN'T BELIEVE REGGIE IS DATING A GIRL FROM A COMPETING BAND!

HEY, TINA! WHAT'S UP?
HOW COOL IS THIS? I'VE BEEN DATING GUYS FROM THREE OF THE BEST BANDS. THEY'RE ALL GONNA TAKE A DIVE FOR ME!
EXIT

WHEN THOSE BANDS GO DOWN, WE'RE SURE TO WIN!
EXIT

SO THAT'S WHY REG DOESN'T HAVE IT TOGETHER!
EXIT
16

THE TRUTH MUST BE TOLD...
GUYS! WAIT'LL YOU HEAR THIS!
POP'S MENU
HEY, POP! CAN I GET SOME BURGERS OVER HERE?
JUG! FORGET THE BURGERS! WHAT'S THE NEWS?!
HEY, ARCH... I DO HAVE PRIORITIES, Y'KNOW?

YOU KNOW THAT REALLY PRETTY GIRL IN THE FALSE STARTS BAND? I THINK HER NAME IS TINA... WELL, I OVERHEARD HER TALKING TO ONE OF HER BANDMATES...
IT'S STOPS AND STARTS. NOW WHAT ABOUT TINA?

SHE SAID SHE'S BEEN DATING BOYS FROM THREE OTHER BANDS, AND CONVINCED THEM TO PLAY BADLY SO THAT SHE COULD WIN THE CONTEST!
!

CAN YOU BELIEVE ANYONE COULD BE SO STUPID AS TO FALL FOR THAT?
HEY! WHERE ARE YOU OFF TO, REG?

COME ON! WE'D BETTER GET PRACTICING! IF TWO OTHER... I MEAN THREE BANDS ARE UNDERMINING THEIR OWN CHANCES... WE STILL HAVE A CHANCE TO WIN!
17

I'M REALLY FEELING IT NOW, ARCH. LET'S GET THIS THING GOING!
NOT SURE WHAT'S COME OVER YOU, REG, BUT I HOPE THE SAME WAVE HAS HIT DILTON!

LIKE I SAID: BRING IT ON!
YOU WERE RIGHT, REG! WELCOME BACK TO THE MUSIC!
The Archies

I THINK I'M GETTING IT NOW, ARCH!
"GETTING IT" MIGHT BE A BIT OPTIMISTIC, BUT YOU ARE GETTING BETTER.
I THINK YOU'RE DOING GREAT, DILTON!

ALRIGHT! I GUESS WE'RE AS READY AS WE'LL EVER BE!
BUT I REALLY HOPE VERONICA MAKES IT HOME IN TIME!
I THINK THIS TRIP'S IN THE BAG!
18

SHOW TIME...

ALRIGHT, ALRIGHT! LET'S SETTLE DOWN! THIS IS AN EXCITING EVENT FOR RIVERDALE HIGH, BUT LET'S TRY TO BE CIVILIZED!

HERE ARE OUR JUDGES--MS. GRUNDY, MR. KRINKLE, MRS. VANHORN, AND MR. CROCKETT!

BRING ON THE BANDS!

LET'S HEAR THE MUSIC!

OK, HERE'S OUR FIRST BAND, THE BLUEBERRY STAINS!

TAKE IT AWAY, YOUNG PEOPLE!

DILTON WAS RIGHT ABOUT THIS BAND! THEY'RE GREAT!

NOW LET'S HEAR-- LEFT REAR POCKET!
THIS BAND IS TOUGH COMPETITION FOR US! THE AUDIENCE LOVES THEM!
OUR ONLY HOPE IS IF DILTON WAS SOMEHOW MAGICALLY TRANS-FORMED OVERNIGHT!
LEFT REAR POCKET
TIME FOR STOPS AND STARTS!
THAT'S TINA!
NO WONDER SHE TRIED TO CHEAT-- THEY STINK!
BOO!!
GET OFF THE STAGE!
THAT GIRL GOT WHAT SHE DESERVED!
BOO!!
AND HERE'S A GROUP WE ALL KNOW-- The ARCHIES!!
THIS IS IT!
LET'S GIVE 'EM WHAT THEY ALL CAME TO HEAR!
OUT OF THE WAY! I HAVE TO GET OUT THERE!
VERONICA!!
20

IT STOPPED SNOWING JUST IN TIME FOR OUR FLIGHT TO TAKE OFF! I'M SO GLAD I MADE IT!
DON'T YOU THINK IT'S A LITTLE LATE TO STEP IN NOW...? I'VE REPLACED YOU WITH DILTON. HE REHEARSED ALL WEEK AND DIDN'T TAKE OFF ON A WHIM!

SO YOU'RE TELLING ME THAT I CAN'T... AFTER I RACED BACK HERE?!
I'M NOT TELLING HIM HE CAN'T PLAY!
SORRY, RON!

I DON'T BELIEVE THIS! FINE! PLAY WITHOUT ME! I'M OUT OF THIS BAND!
I HOPE VERONICA'S OK!
SHE JUST NEEDS TIME TO COOL OFF!

ALRIGHT, THEN! EVERYBODY READY TO ROCK-N-ROLL?!
LET'S PLAY LIKE THERE'S NO TOMORROW!
I WON'T LET YOU DOWN, ARCH!
I REALLY THINK WE CAN WIN THIS THING!!
21

AND THE WINNERS OF THE BATTLE OF THE BANDS COMPETITION ARE...
PLEASE BE US!
I HOPE I WAS WRONG ABOUT THE WHOLE BAD KARMA THING!
I FEEL REALLY GOOD ABOUT THIS!
I HOPE WE WIN... JUST TO SEE TINA'S FACE!
JUG
OH! THERE ARE TWO WINNERS! IT'S A TIE BETWEEN LEFT REAR POCKET AND THE ARCHIES!
LET'S GET BOTH THESE BANDS BACK ON STAGE!!
LET'S JAM!!
YOU SEE, JUGGIE? WE HAD HALF GOOD KARMA AND NOW A WHOLE GREAT TRIP!
SUN AND SURF, HERE WE COME!!
LEFT REAR POCKET
END PART ONE

IN OUR LAST EPISODE...
IT'S TIME FOR RIVERDALE HIGH'S BATTLE OF THE BANDS, SPONSORED BY THE RIVERDALE MUSIC EMPORIUM...
DID YOU ALL HEAR ABOUT THE BATTLE OF THE BANDS? THE ARCHIES CAN WIN THAT NO PROBLEM--AND THE GRAND PRIZE IS A TRIP TO HAWAII!!
POP'S
POP'S
BUT ARCHIE'S IN FOR A SHOCK WHEN HE HEARS THE OTHER BANDS...
WE TAPED YOUR COMPETITION FOR THE COMPETITION!
LISTEN TO THIS!
DADDY HAS GREAT NEWS! THE FORECAST CALLS FOR FRESH SNOW IN COLORADO. AND SINCE WE'RE ON VACATION--WE'RE GOING SKIING!!
SKIING?! BUT WHAT ABOUT REHEARSALS?!
SORRY, ARCH, BUT VERONICA'S STUCK IN A SNOW STORM AND WON'T BE BACK FOR THE CONTEST!
WHAT?
LUCKILY, DILTON WAS THERE TO STEP IN FOR VERONICA...
ALRIGHT--EVERYBODY READY TO ROCK 'N' ROLL?!
I WON'T LET YOU DOWN, ARCH!
Oh! I SEE THERE ARE TWO WINNERS! IT'S A TIE BETWEEN THE LEFT REAR POCKET AND--
--the ARCHIES!!
1

BATTLE OF THE BANDS PART TWO:
BAND TRIP
STARRING THE Archies
SUN AND FUN, HERE WE COME!!
ALL EXPENSES PAID TRIP TO HAWAII!! YES!!
IT DOESN'T GET BETTER THAN THIS!
I'VE BEEN LOOKING FOR YOU, ARCHIE.
MR. WEATHERBEE WANTS TO SEE YOU RIGHT AWAY!
OK, MS. GRUNDY... I'LL BE RIGHT THERE!
THE BEE PROBABLY WANTS TO FILL ME IN ON THE TRIP DETAILS!
ASK IF WE CAN FLY FIRST CLASS!
2

SO WHAT'S UP, MR. WEATHERBEE? WANT TO FILL ME IN ON OUR FLIGHT AND HOTEL INFO?
NOT EXACTLY...

I SPOKE WITH THE TRIP SPONSOR, AND...

LATER THAT AFTERNOON...
SO WHAT DID THE BEE HAVE TO SAY, ARCHIE?
DID HE TELL YOU ABOUT OUR HOTEL?
POP'S
POP'S

NO, HE DIDN'T GIVE ME ANY TRIP DETAILS.
THEN WHAT DID HE SAY? THE TRIP'S STILL ON, ISN'T IT?

YEAH ... BUT THERE'S A SLIGHT PROBLEM, THOUGH.
POP'S

THE SPONSOR ONLY AGREED TO PAY FOR ONE BAND'S TRIP. NOW THAT THERE ARE TWO BANDS, WE ALL HAVE TO PAY FOR HALF OF THE TRIP!
3

WHAT?!

OH, IS THAT ALL? I'M SURE MY DAD WILL COVER MY HALF!
THAT'S EASY FOR YOU TO SAY, BUT HOW ARE THE REST OF US GOING TO PAY FOR THIS?

THE TRIP'S IN TWO WEEKS!
HOW WILL WE EVER RAISE THE MONEY IN TIME?
POP'S

CALM DOWN! WE CAN FIGURE THIS OUT. LET'S THINK OF SOME JOBS WE CAN DO TO EARN MONEY!
POP'S
POP'S
RIVERDAL

ARCHIE'S RIGHT. WE CAN THINK OF SOME-THING!
ALL RIGHT, I GUESS!
THAT'S THE SPIRIT! MEET ME AT MY HOUSE TONIGHT WITH YOUR IDEAS. WE CAN'T WASTE ANY TIME!
HEY! HAS ANYONE SEEN VERONICA? SHE STILL DOESN'T KNOW SHE CAN COME WITH US TO HAWAII!
I HAVEN'T HEARD FROM HER. I THINK SHE'S STILL UPSET THAT YOU WOULDN'T LET HER PLAY IN THE COM-PETITION!
POP'S MENU
4

HELLO, ARCHIE. I'LL LET MS. VERONICA KNOW YOU'RE HERE.
HI, RON!
WHAT'RE YOU DOING HERE?
RIVERDALE
WELL, WE HAVEN'T SEEN YOU AROUND, SO I THOUGHT I'D CHECK UP ON YOU!
I'VE BEEN BUSY. BESIDES, YOU DIDN'T SEEM TO NEED ME AT THE BATTLE OF THE BANDS!
R

AWW, COME ON, RON! YOU GOTTA UNDERSTAND WHY I HAD TO DO THAT!

IF YOU COULD JUST PUT THIS BEHIND YOU. I WANT YOU TO COME WITH US ON THE TRIP! WE'RE GOING TO HAWAII!

I GUESS IT WOULD BE FUN TO GO TO HAWAII! BUT THIS DOESN'T MEAN I'M OVER THIS!
EXCELLENT!!
OH, ONE OTHER THING. SINCE THERE ARE TWO BANDS GOING, WE EACH HAVE TO PAY FOR HALF THE TRIP!
R

THAT WON'T BE A PROBLEM!
IT IS FOR SOME OF US! WE'RE MEETING AT MY HOUSE TONIGHT TO DISCUSS IT!
R
5

THAT NIGHT...
ALL RIGHT THEN. WHAT IDEAS DO WE HAVE?

I GOT A GREAT BABY-SITTING JOB. FIVE KIDS, AND THEY'RE PAYING ME LOTS TO WATCH THEM ALL!

I HAVE A NEW EFFICIENCY MACHINE THAT I'M GOING TO TRY TO SELL TO THE ACME DOLL COMPANY!

I HEARD THEY'RE LOOKING FOR SOME-ONE AT THE BAKERY. I'M GOING TO CHECK IT OUT TOMORROW!

THEY NEED A DELIVERY BOY AT THE PIZZA PARLOR. THAT SOUNDS JUST RIGHT FOR ME.

I KNEW WE COULD DO THIS! LET'S GO FOR IT!!
6

THE NEXT DAY, JUGHEAD MOVES FROM BURGERS TO BAKED GOODS...
I THINK WE'VE COVERED EVERY-THING, JUGHEAD. JUST ONE LAST THING...
BEST BAKERS

DON'T EAT ANY CAKE WHILE YOU'RE WORKING.
NO PROBLEM!

ENJOY!

IT CAN'T HURT TO SAMPLE THE FROSTING.

BEST BAKERS
I'D RATHER EAT BURGERS ANYWAY!
7

THEY SHOULDN'T BE ANY TROUBLE!
DON'T WORRY ABOUT US! HAVE A GREAT TIME!
27

OK, WHAT WOULD EVERYONE LIKE TO DO? PLAY A GAME OR WATCH A MOVIE?

HEY! WHAT'S GOING ON?!

IT'S ALL RIGHT, MOMMY WILL BE HOME SOON! DON'T CRY!
AND THE REST OF YOU, STOP THIS FOOD FIGHT RIGHT NOW!

ZZZZZZZZZZZZZZZZZZZZZZZ
8

THE SALE OF DILTON'S NEW MACHINE WILL MORE THAN PAY FOR HIS TRIP.
THIS OUGHTA DO IT! THEN WE'LL BE GOOD TO GO!

HIT THE SWITCH, MR. NEWSOME!

I HAVE TO ADMIT, I HAD MY DOUBTS, BUT THIS MACHINE IS TERRIFIC!

WH-WHAT'S HAPPENING?!

DON'T WORRY, MR. NEWSOME! EVERYTHING'S UNDER CONTROL! THE MACHINE JUST NEEDS AN ADJUSTMENT OR TWO...

...OR NOT.
9

FILL OUT THIS APPLICATION, AND THEN BRING IT BACK TO ME.
YOU GOT IT!
PIZZA KING
RIV

HOWYA DOING? ARE YOU APPLYING FOR THE PIZZA DELIVERY JOB, TOO?
YEAH, I AM! I REALLY NEED THIS JOB!

WAIT A MINUTE! AREN'T YOU JOE CALLAHAN? YOU'RE CAPTAIN OF THE TRACK TEAM!
WAS CAPTAIN. I HAD TO QUIT THE TEAM WHEN MY DAD LOST HIS JOB. WE COULD LOSE OUR HOUSE, SO THE ONLY PLACE I'LL BE RUNNING IS AROUND TOWN WITH PIZZA... IF I LAND THE JOB!

ARE YOU BOYS DONE WITH THOSE APPLICATIONS? I'M SORRY, BUT I CAN ONLY HIRE ONE OF YOU!
MAN... THIS KID NEEDS THE JOB MORE THAN I DO!
PIZZA KING

ON SECOND THOUGHT, THIS JOB ISN'T REALLY WHAT I WAS LOOKING FOR. SEE YOU AROUND, JOE!
PIZZA KING
R
TRASH
PIZZA KING
10

THAT NIGHT...
SO... HOW ARE THE JOBS GOING?
MINE WAS A BIG DISASTER. THE KIDS WERE MONSTERS! I'M NOT GOING BACK!

MINE WAS GREAT UNTIL MY MACHINE HAD A SLIGHT... er... OK, MAJOR MAL-FUNCTION!

I'M NOT CUT OUT FOR FOOD SALES!

WOULDN'T YOU KNOW ANOTHER KID APPLIED FOR THE JOB I WANTED AND HE NEEDED IT WAY MORE THAN ME!

SO WHAT WILL YOU DO NOW?

11

I DO HAVE ONE
MORE POSSIBILITY.

UNUSUAL JOBS!
OPEN
SPACES &
GREAT PAY!!
Call: 1-555-REAL JOB
FOR DETAILS

WOW! THIS SOUNDS
GREAT!!

LET'S CHECK
THIS OUT!

REAL JOBS.
HOW CAN I
HELP YOU?
REAL
J$BS
12

I SAW YOUR AD IN THE PAPER. DO YOU HAVE ANY POSITIONS LEFT?
WE SURE DO! WHEN CAN YOU START?
JOBS

ACTUALLY, IT'S NOT JUST ME. THERE ARE FOUR OF US LOOKING FOR WORK. ANY CHANCE YOU HAVE FOUR SPOTS?
YES! WE DO! ALL OF YOU CAN COME DOWN TO OUR OFFICE TOMORROW TO FILL OUT SOME FORMS AND YOU CAN GET STARTED RIGHT AWAY!
ARE YOU SURE ABOUT THIS? HE'S NEVER MET YOU AND HE'S READY TO HIRE YOU ALL?

HE PROBABLY COULD TELL FROM MY VOICE THAT I'M A DECENT GUY. ANYWAY, WE NEED THESE JOBS AND WE'RE TAKING THEM!
IT'S EASY FOR YOU TO JUDGE WHEN YOU DON'T NEED A JOB. THIS SOUNDS LIKE AN OPPORTUNITY! I SAY WE GO FOR IT!!

HAWAII, HERE WE COME!
YOU SAID IT, DILTY!
YES!
13

TH-THIS IS DISGUSTING!
I'M BEGINNING TO SEE WHY ANYONE COULD HAVE THIS JO--
--B!
SPLOOT
COME ON, GUYS! IT'S ONLY FOR A COUPLE OF WEEKS... THEN WE'RE OFF TO FUN IN THE SUN!
GLOOSH
14

WHATEVER I THOUGHT ABOUT PARTY RENTALS, I NEVER THOUGHT ABOUT THE CLEAN-UP AFTERWARDS!
PARTY RENT
OPEN

I'M GAGGING ON THIS, JUG!
THINK OF THE TRIP, BETTY!

LOOK AT THE BRIGHT SIDE. THIS STEAM WILL CLEAR OUR LUNGS!

MAYBE YOU SHOULD TRY SCRAPING THOSE DISHES, AND I'LL CLEAR MY LUNGS OVER HERE!

C'MON, BETTY! WATCH OUT!!
CUT IT OUT, GUYS! WE HAVE TO GET BACK TO WORK!
SOAP SUDS

15

ALL OF THIS GARBAGE HAS TO BE CLEANED UP BEFORE THE GAME THIS AFTERNOON!
EXIT
RIVERDALE
VISITORS

DOESN'T ANYONE USE A GARBAGE CAN?

I DON'T WANT TO KNOW WHAT THIS IS!
TRASH

AAAGHH!!

SO THIS IS THE WORK YOU FOUND? I SEE YOU'VE GOT THE OPEN SPACES COVERED. AND IT'S DEFINITELY HONEST WORK. BUT I WOULDN'T CALL IT A CLEAN LIVING!

AT LEAST WE'RE LEARNING THE MEANING OF EARNING SOME-THING!
THAT'S TRUE! I GUESS I'LL HAVE TO LEARN THINGS THE EASY WAY!
16

REGGIE LAUGHED ALL THE WAY HOME...
HI, SON!
HI, DAD!

WHAT'S SO FUNNY?
OH, ARCHIE AND EVERYBODY ELSE HAVE TO RAISE MONEY FOR OUR BAND TRIP, AND THEY ENDED UP WITH A REALLY GROSS JOB!

IT WAS SO FUNNY TO SEE THEM KNEE DEEP IN GARBAGE!
MILK
SO LET ME GET THIS STRAIGHT... YOU FIND THEIR HONEST, HARD WORK AMUSING?

WELL... YEAH...!
INTERESTING.

YOU KNOW, I HAD TO DO MY SHARE OF HARD WORK TO GET WHERE I AM TODAY!
17

I KNOW, I KNOW! YOU STARTED AT THE BOTTOM AND EVEN WALKED FIVE MILES TO SCHOOL--IN THE SNOW! YOU TOLD ME A HUNDRED TIMES!

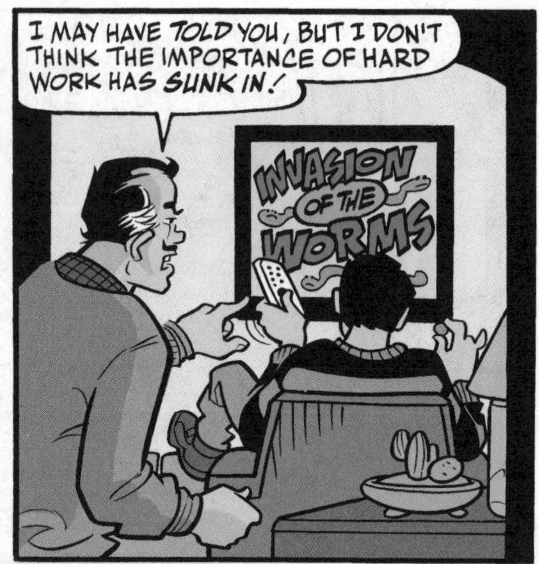
I MAY HAVE TOLD YOU, BUT I DON'T THINK THE IMPORTANCE OF HARD WORK HAS SUNK IN!
INVASION OF THE WORMS

HEY! WHAT'RE YOU DOING?!
REGGIE, I THINK IT'S TIME YOU GOT A JOB!
BLIB
KLIK

WHAT?!
IN FACT, I THINK IT WOULD DO YOU A WORLD OF GOOD TO RAISE THE MONEY FOR YOUR TRIP!

NO WAY!! I WOULDN'T EVEN KNOW WHERE TO LOOK FOR A JOB!
WELL, I DO!
18

SO...YOU WONDERED WHERE THE FLOWERS FROM THE RIVERDALE FLORAL PARADE WENT. THEY ALL LANDED HERE IN MY WAREHOUSE. NOW THEY HAVE TO BE BAGGED AND SENT OUT!

I CAN'T BELIEVE MY FATHER IS MAKING ME DO THIS!
I DON'T THINK I CAN DO THIS!
RIVERDALE

BETTY, I KNOW THIS IS REALLY GROSS, BUT WE'VE GOT TO HANG IN THERE! IT'S JUST A LITTLE LONGER, AND WE'LL BE IN THE SUN!
THIS IS ONE PLACE A ROSE DOESN'T SMELL LIKE A ROSE

I'M TRYING, ARCH... BUT IT SMELLS SO BAD IN HERE FROM THE ROTTING FLOWERS! I'M GETTING SICK!
HANG ON, BETTY! MY PHONE'S RINGING!

HELLO? MR. WEATHERBEE!

THE TRIP OPERATOR WANTS TO KNOW IF THE TRIP IS STILL ON, ARCHIE. CAN YOU RAISE THE MONEY?
YOU ONLY HAVE ONE MORE DAY!
19

DON'T WORRY, MR. WEATHERBEE! NO PROBLEMS HERE. WE'VE GOT THE MONEY... SEE YOU AT THE AIRPORT!

OK, GANG, WE ONLY HAVE ONE DAY TO EARN THE REST OF THE MONEY! WE'D BETTER GET MOVING!

ARCH, I--I CAN'T DO THIS ANYMORE! I JUST CAN'T. I'M REALLY FEELING SICK! I'M SO SORRY. I HOPE YOU CAN FINISH THE JOB WITHOUT ME!
DON'T WORRY, BETTY... I'LL FIGURE SOME-THING OUT!

WHAT DO I DO NOW?

IT'S A LONG SHOT, BUT MAYBE IT'LL WORK!

OH, PLEASE! YOU JUST GOTTA HELP US! IF WE DON'T FINISH THIS BY TOMORROW, WE WON'T GO ON THE TRIP!

20

VERONICA! WHAT'RE YOU DOING HERE?!
I'M ASKING MYSELF THAT SAME QUESTION!
ACM WAREH

THERE'S NO WAY WE COULD FINISH THIS WITHOUT BETTY, SO VERONICA AGREED TO HELP OUT!
AND BOY DO YOU OWE ME! I HAD NO IDEA IT WOULD BE THIS DISGUSTING!
LET'S GET GOING... WE HAVE NO TIME TO WASTE!

21

24 HOURS LATER...

HURRY! THE PLANE IS LEAVING IN FIVE MINUTES!

FLIGHT 9 HAWAII

HAWAII

YOU MADE IT!!! I WAS GETTING NERVOUS! THE OTHER BAND IS ALREADY HERE... THEY'RE SITTING IN THE BACK.

I HAD TO WORK YOUR JOB UNTIL ABOUT AN HOUR AGO!

YEAH! WE COULDN'T GET PAID UNTIL THE JOB WAS DONE!

TIME

SORRY ABOUT THAT! BUT I'M FEELING MUCH BETTER NOW, AND...

...I KNOW I'M LOOKING FORWARD TO HAVING TONS OF FUN WITH YOU...

The Archies IN NEW YORK

WOW! HERE WE ARE IN NEW YORK CITY! FOR OUR FIRST GIG!

HOW EXCITING!

I CAN'T WAIT TO GO SHOPPING ON 5TH AVENUE!

I'LL BET YOUR SUITCASE IS FULL OF CREDIT CARDS!

LOOK AT ALL OUR FANS WHO SHOWED UP!

WE ♥ THE ARCHIES

WELCOME ARCHIES

LOOK! THERE'S THE STRETCH LIMO DADDY SENT FOR US! HE WANTED US TO ARRIVE IN STYLE!
WOW! WHAT A MOB SCENE!
EVER SINCE OUR NEW SMASH RECORD "EVERYTHING'S ALRIGHT" HIT THE TOP TEN, IT'S BEEN A WILD RIDE!

GOSH! THE TRAFFIC IS SO CRAZY!
I COULD RUN FASTER THAN WE ARE DRIVING...!
ACM
THERE ARE PEOPLE RUNNING FASTER THAN WE ARE DRIVING!
NEW YORKERS ARE TRUE SURVIVORS!

I'M GETTING HUNGRY JUST WATCHING THEM! LET'S PULL OVER FOR A QUICK SLICE?
PIZZA
$3
SLICE

WOW! EVERYTHING IS BIGGER AND BETTER IN NEW YORK IT SEEMS!
2

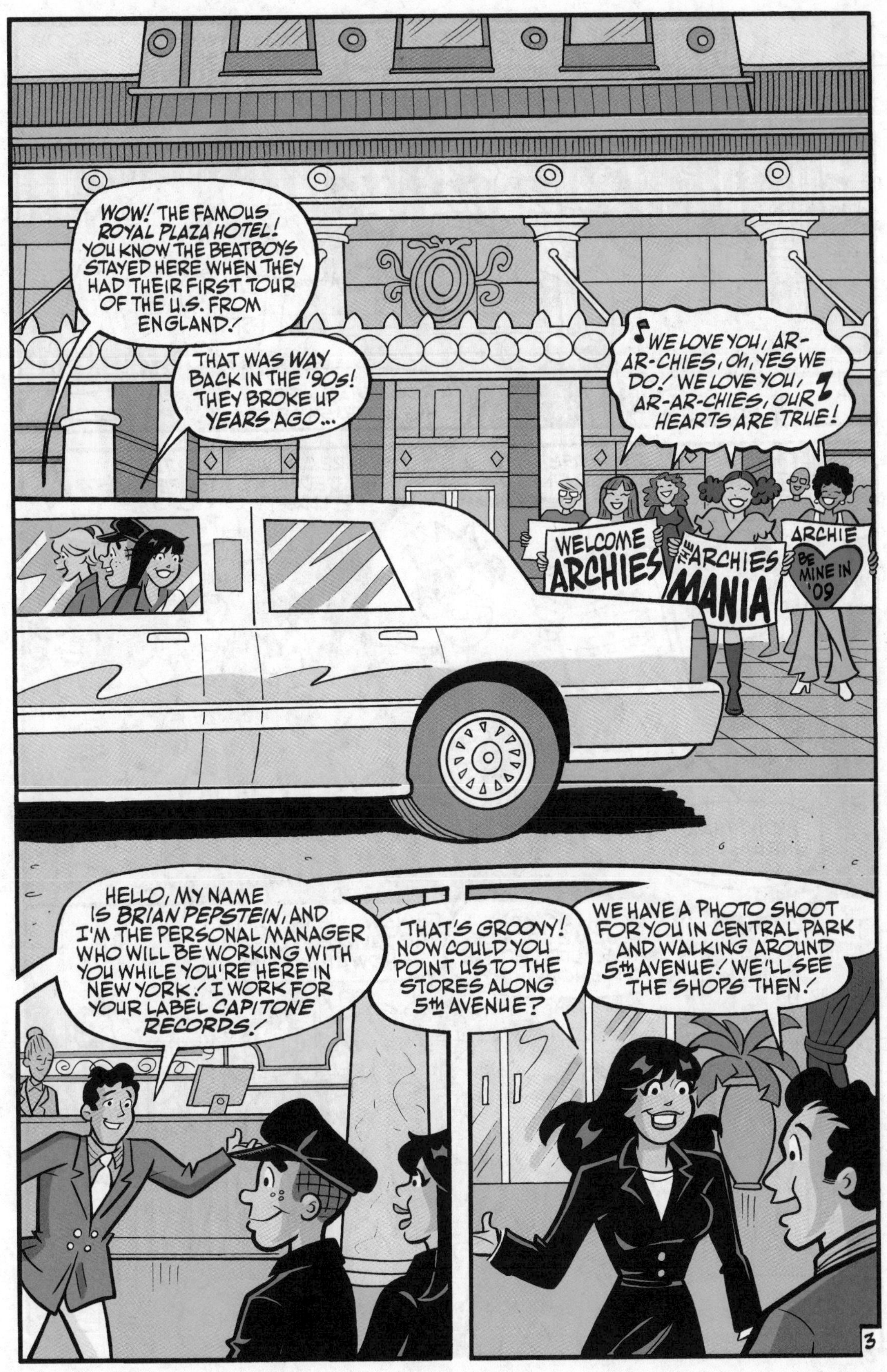
WOW! THE FAMOUS ROYAL PLAZA HOTEL! YOU KNOW THE BEATBOYS STAYED HERE WHEN THEY HAD THEIR FIRST TOUR OF THE U.S. FROM ENGLAND!
THAT WAS WAY BACK IN THE '90s! THEY BROKE UP YEARS AGO...
WE LOVE YOU, AR-AR-CHIES, OH, YES WE DO! WE LOVE YOU, AR-AR-CHIES, OUR HEARTS ARE TRUE!
WELCOME ARCHIES
THE ARCHIES MANIA
ARCHIE BE MINE IN '09
HELLO, MY NAME IS BRIAN PEPSTEIN, AND I'M THE PERSONAL MANAGER WHO WILL BE WORKING WITH YOU WHILE YOU'RE HERE IN NEW YORK! I WORK FOR YOUR LABEL CAPITONE RECORDS!
THAT'S GROOVY! NOW COULD YOU POINT US TO THE STORES ALONG 5th AVENUE?
WE HAVE A PHOTO SHOOT FOR YOU IN CENTRAL PARK AND WALKING AROUND 5th AVENUE! WE'LL SEE THE SHOPS THEN!
3

HEY, THIS IS ONE FANCY HOTEL SUITE!
ARE YOU KIDDING? DON'T YOU LIVE LIKE THIS ALL THE TIME?
ACTUALLY, I DO!
WHERE'S THE ROOM SERVICE? I'VE ORDERED A GRILLED CHEESE SANDWICH AND SOME FRUIT COCKTAIL!
A ROCK STAR NEEDS HIS NOURISHMENT!
HEY, LOOK GANG! "EVERYTHING'S ALRIGHT" JUST HIT NUMBER ONE ON BILLBORE'S TOP 40 POP CHART!
TOP 40
WOW! THAT'S UNREAL! HOW COOL!
WHERE ARE WE HEADED NOW, FELLAS?
"TO THE TOPPERMOST OF THE POPPERMOST!"
GOSH! SO MANY AWESOME STORES AND SO LITTLE TIME FOR SHOPPING!
I KNOW... WE'RE TAPING THE DAVID BETTERMAN SHOW AT 5:00PM!
I CAN'T BELIEVE WE'RE GOING TO BE ON THAT SHOW!
KEEP SNAPPING, BLOKES!
4

OKAY, WE'RE IN CENTRAL PARK NOW... WANT TO GET SOME PUBLICITY SHOTS HERE ?
HEY, THIS IS REALLY COOL! IT'S LIKE BEING A KID AGAIN!
WHO EVER STOPPED BEING ONE!
WELL, BETS... LIFE SURE HAS ITS UPS AND DOWNS!
HA! HA!
QUIT HORSING AROUND, RONNIE!
HEY, THESE GUYS KEEP A MEAN BEAT GOING!
YOU GOT THE GROOVE, JUG! ROCK STEADY, BRO!

OKAY, KIDS! WE GOTTA GO SOON.!
GIVE SOME MORE PROMO COPIES OF THE ARCHIES' NEW CD TO THE KIDS!

OKAY, NOW WE'RE HEADED TO LUNCH AT THE WORLD FAMOUS "TAVERN ON THE GREEN" HERE IN CENTRAL PARK!
Tavern on the Green
5

CAN'T WAIT TO HAVE SOME OF THOSE FAMOUS MARYLAND CRAB CAKES!
HOW 'BOUT THAT PORTER-HOUSE BACON CHEESE-BURGER? AND FRIES? YES, PLEASE!

AND THE BEST NEWS OF ALL... CAPITONE RECORDS IS PAYING THE TAB -- SO ORDER UP!
HAVING A HIT RECORD HAS ITS PERKS!
I CAN'T BELIEVE THIS MENU! HOW DEE-LISH! A FRESH MEDITERRANEAN SALAD WITH FETA CHEESE, OLIVES, CAPERS AND A HARD-BOILED EGG! THAT SOUNDS LIKE THE PERFECT PROTEIN BUILD-UP FOR TONIGHT'S TV TAPING!
I WANT TO TAKE SOME OF THEIR KILLER FRENCH FRIES BACK TO THE HOTEL --
Tavern on the Green
Tavern on the Green
-- FOR A BEDTIME SNACK!

THANKS, MS. SMITH! WE'D BE HONORED TO HAVE YOU WRITE ABOUT US!
THE ARCHIES ARE THE ONLY POP GROUP I LISTEN TO! YOU'RE THE BEST THING SINCE *FRANK SUMATRA!*
WHAT A DAY! LET'S HEAD BACK TO THE HOTEL... I WANT TO GO OVER THE SONGS FOR TONIGHT'S SHOW!
I'M GOING TO WALK BACK! I WANT TO FIT INTO MY OUTFIT TONIGHT!
I'LL JOIN YOU!
LATER, GUYS!
7

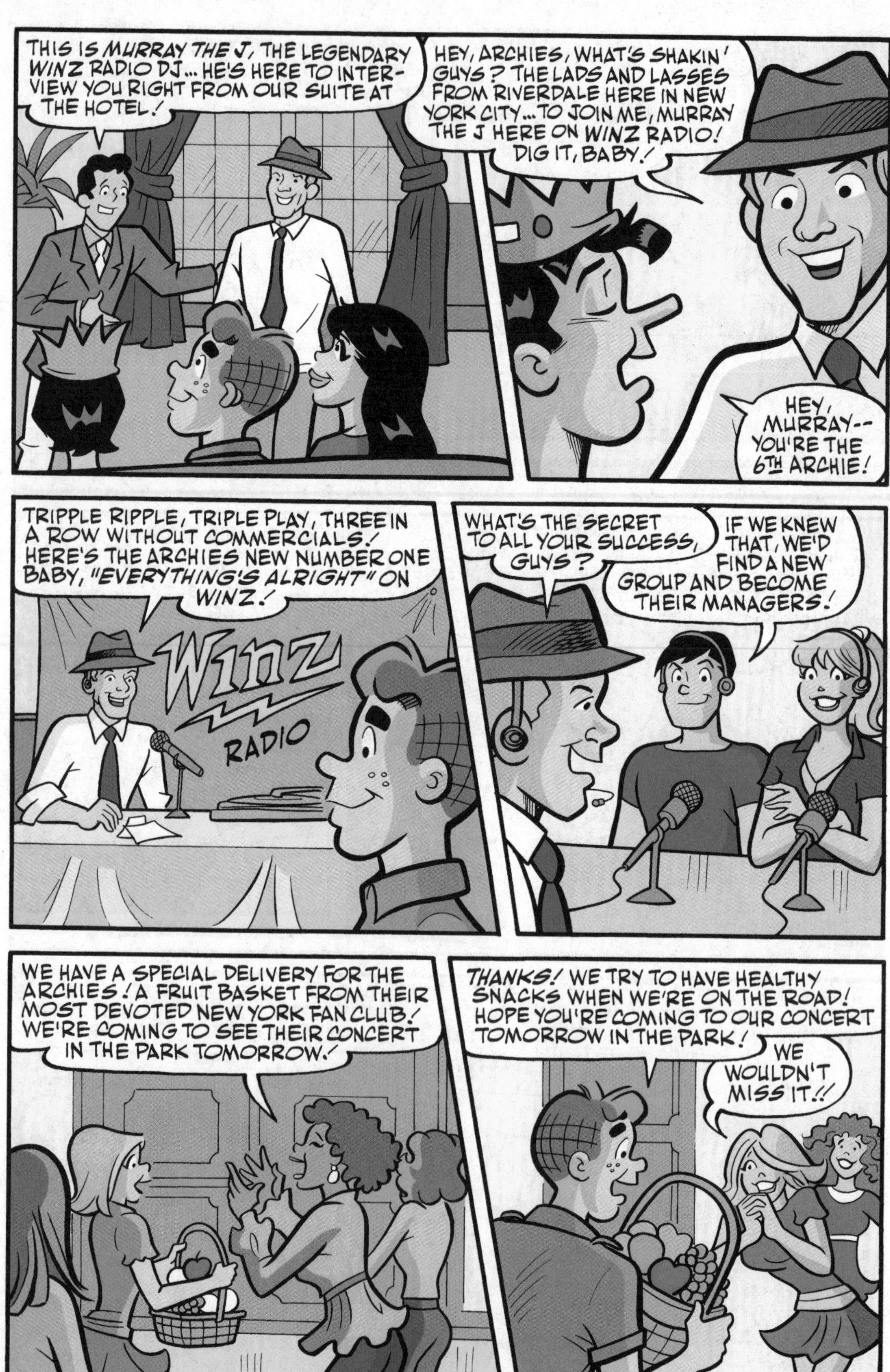
THIS IS MURRAY THE J, THE LEGENDARY WINZ RADIO DJ... HE'S HERE TO INTERVIEW YOU RIGHT FROM OUR SUITE AT THE HOTEL!
HEY, ARCHIES, WHAT'S SHAKIN' GUYS? THE LADS AND LASSES FROM RIVERDALE HERE IN NEW YORK CITY... TO JOIN ME, MURRAY THE J HERE ON WINZ RADIO! DIG IT, BABY!
HEY, MURRAY-- YOU'RE THE 6TH ARCHIE!
TRIPPLE RIPPLE, TRIPLE PLAY, THREE IN A ROW WITHOUT COMMERCIALS! HERE'S THE ARCHIES NEW NUMBER ONE BABY, "EVERYTHING'S ALRIGHT" ON WINZ!
WINZ
RADIO
WHAT'S THE SECRET TO ALL YOUR SUCCESS, GUYS?
IF WE KNEW THAT, WE'D FIND A NEW GROUP AND BECOME THEIR MANAGERS!
WE HAVE A SPECIAL DELIVERY FOR THE ARCHIES! A FRUIT BASKET FROM THEIR MOST DEVOTED NEW YORK FAN CLUB! WE'RE COMING TO SEE THEIR CONCERT IN THE PARK TOMORROW!
THANKS! WE TRY TO HAVE HEALTHY SNACKS WHEN WE'RE ON THE ROAD! HOPE YOU'RE COMING TO OUR CONCERT TOMORROW IN THE PARK!
WE WOULDN'T MISS IT!!
8

LET'S GO GANG! WE DON'T WANT TO BE LATE... AND BRING YOUR JACKETS, I HEAR MR. BETTERMAN KEEPS THE STUDIO AT A CHILLY 65 DEGREES FOR THE TAPING!
THERE IT IS! THE FAMOUS ED SULLIMAN THEATER! THE BEATBOYS PLAYED HERE WHEN THEY MADE THEIR TV DEBUT IN THE U.S.!
Ed Sulliman THEATE
WELL, GOSH KIDS! WE'RE VERY EXCITED TO HAVE AMERICA'S HOTTEST GROUP ON TONIGHT... HERE TO PEFORM THEIR NEW NUMBER ONE RECORD, "EVERYTHING'S ALRIGHT"... LADIES AND GENTLEMEN-- The ARCHIES!
"IN THE PARK ON SUNDAY, HAND IN HAND ON SUNDAY... WATCHING THE CHILDREN PLAY... I BUY SOME CANDY, SOME SWEET SWEET CANDY... DON'TCHA' LOVE THE SUNSHINE DAY? EVERY-THING'S ALRIGHT WITH ME... EVERYTHING'S ALRIGHT, ALRIGHT, ALRIGHT!
The Archies
"THAT'S THE WAY IT SHOULD BE!"
THE ARCHIES ARE SO FAB!
ROCK ON, JUGHEAD!
LET'S HEAR IT FOR The ARCHIES!! ALL THE WAY FROM RIVERDALE! AND THEY'LL BE DOING A FREE BENEFIT CONCERT FOR THE NEW YORK HOMELESS SHELTER IN CENTRAL PARK TOMORROW!
9

THE NEXT DAY...

I LOVE WEARING OUR STAGE OUTFITS! WHY CAN'T WE DRESS LIKE THIS **ALL** THE TIME!

YOU MEAN YOU **DON'T**?

WHAT MADE YOU JOIN THE ARCHIES, JUGHEAD?
WELL, IT WAS MAINLY THAT ARCHIE AND REGGIE WANTED TO BE IN FRONT AND I DIDN'T MIND BEING IN BACK! PLUS, I CAN HIDE SOME SNACKS BEHIND MY DRUM KIT ON STAGE!
JUGGIE, WE ARE SO LATE FOR THE SHOW! WE GOTTA GO!
THIS ISN'T THE KIND OF ROCK STAR YOU NEED TO BE!
PUT THOSE PEBBLES DOWN AND LET'S GET CRACKIN'!

GOOD THING YOU CAN RELY ON NEW YORK'S CAB DRIVERS TO GET YOU WHERE YOU NEED TO GO IN A HURRY!
I'LL SAY! IT'S EARLIER THAN WHEN WE LEFT THE HOTEL!
TAXI
LET'S GO GUYS! NOT A MINUTE TO LOSE! THE SHOW'S ABOUT TO START!
TAXI
WESTSIDE
HOMELESS SHELTER
WHAT WOULD WE DO WITHOUT ROCK'N'ROLL MUSIC? ROCK'N'ROLL MUSIC MAKES YOU FEEL ALL RIGHT! FEEL ALL RIGHT! FEEL ALL RIGHT ALL NIGHT!
The ARCHIES
WE LOVE YOU BETTY!
The ARCHIES ROCK!
VERONICA IS WAY COOL!
11

IT'S STARTING TO RAIN!
I KNOW! THERE GOES MY HAIR! BUT THE SHOW MUST GO ON!
OKAY, EVERY-BODY--!

WE'RE NOT GOING TO LET A LITTLE RAIN STOP US, RIGHT? WE'RE IN NEW YORK! THE SHOW MUST GO ON!!

WE WON'T LET A LITTLE RAIN SPOIL OUR CONCERT! WE'RE NEW YORKERS! WE CAN DEAL WITH ANY TYPE OF WEATHER!
YEAH!
ROCK ON!!

WE HAVE A SPECIAL GUEST HERE TO JOIN THE SHOW! EVERY-BODY WELCOME-- MISS DIANA BOSS!
REACH OUT AN TOUCH SOMEBODY'S HAND... MAKE THIS WORLD A BETTER PLACE IF YOU CAN!
WHAT A GREAT TRIP TO NEW YORK THIS HAS BEEN! I CAN'T WAIT TO COME BACK AGAIN! IT'S THE GREATEST CITY IN THE WORLD!!
EXCEPT FOR RIVERDALE, THAT IS!
END

CHAPTER SIX

The 2010s

ARCHIE IN
BANDED TOGETHER!
SEPTEMBER 2011

SCRIPT: DAN PARENT PENCILS: FERNANDO RUIZ INKS: RICH KOSLOWSKI
LETTERS: JACK MORELLI COLORS: DIGIKORE STUDIOS

THE ARCHIES IN
SEND IN THE CLOWNS!
NOVEMBER 2011

SCRIPT: ALEX SIMMONS PENCILS: DAN PARENT INKS: RICH KOSLOWSKI
LETTERS: JACK MORELLI COLORS: DIGIKORE STUDIOS

THE ARCHIES IN
THE ARCHIES ROCKIN' WORLD TOUR

PART 1: BOLLYWOOD LOVE!
JANUARY 2014

PART 2: LOVE ON THE ROAD
FEBRUARY 2014

PART 3: BLUNDER DOWN UNDER
MARCH 2014

PART 4: CLOSE TO THE BORDERLINE
APRIL 2014

SCRIPT & PENCILS: DAN PARENT INKS: RICH KOSLOWSKI
LETTERS: JACK MORELLI COLORS: DIGIKORE STUDIOS

ARCHIE IN
banded TOGETHER!
VERONICA! YOU'RE LATE FOR PRACTICE... AGAIN!
THAT'S BECAUSE I WAS BUSY WATCHING "POP-TV"! QUICK, TURN ON THE TV! YOU WON'T BELIEVE THE NEWS!
YOU HEARD IT HERE! SIMON COWELL WILL BE LEAVING AMERICAN IDOL AND STARTING HIS OWN TALENT COMPETITION CALLED "The X FACTOR"!
POP TV
1

WOW! AMERICAN IDOL IS THE #1 SHOW ON TV!
THEY'LL NEVER REPLACE HIM! HE'S THE BEST JUDGE ON THE SHOW!
SIMON HAS ALREADY BEEN RE-PLACED!
WELL, THAT WAS FAST!
HIS REPLACEMENT IS POP SENSATION J. LO!
J. LO??! EVERYBODY KNOWS THEY CAN'T STAND EACH OTHER!
REMEMBER, IT ALL STARTED WHEN J. LO WAS A CONTESTANT ON THE SHOW!
"SIMON HUMILIATED HER, TELLING HER SHE'D NEVER GET ANYWHERE!
"SO, SHE LEFT IN A RAGE! AND WITH A LOT OF MONEY, AMBITION AND AUTO-TUNE, SHE LEAPT TO STARDOM!"
WOW
J. LO!!
STYLE
J. LO!!
J. LO!
J. LO'S BACK!
2

"EVEN WITH HER SUCCESS, SIMON STILL SLAMMED HER!
"AND J. LO TOOK DIGS AT SIMON WHENEVER SHE COULD!"
I'D LIKE TO NOT THANK SIMON FOR THIS AWARD!
IN FACT, I'D LIKE TO CLUB HIM OVER THE HEAD WITH IT.!!
AND NOW, WITH EACH CELEBRITY HEADLINING DIFFERENT COMPETITION SHOWS -- THE BATTLE IS ON.!!
WE NEED TO GET ON ONE OF THESE SHOWS! THE EXPOSURE WILL BE PHENOMENAL!
WE'RE ALREADY SUCCESSFUL! WE HAVE A RECORDING CONTRACT!
I'M TALKING ABOUT THE FINALE! WHERE POPULAR BANDS PERFORM BEFORE THEY ANNOUNCE THE WINNER!
3

THOSE BANDS' SALES SKYROCKET AFTER THESE SHOWS!
LET'S SEE IF WE CAN GET ON ONE OF THEM!
I'LL CALL MARCY AND GET HER ON THE JOB!
LATER...
GOOD NEWS! "X FACTOR" IS VERY INTERESTED!
GREAT!
BUT ONE THING...
YOU HAVE TO AUDITION FOR SIMON!
WHAT?! BUT WE'RE ALREADY A SUCCESSFUL BAND!
IT DOESN'T MATTER! ALL THE BANDS THAT WANT TO BE ON THE FINALE HAVE TO AUDITION!
SO!
THIS IS HUMILIATING, HAVING TO AUDITION!
DON'T FEEL BAD! WE'RE IN GOOD COMPANY!
IS THAT--
FACTOR
4

-- The ROLLING STONES!
AND AEROSMITH! WOW!
LET'S GO! WE'RE UP!
HI, SIMON! NICE TO MEET YOU!
THAT'S MR. COWELL TO YOU!
hmph!
WHAT WOULD YOU LIKE TO HEAR?
SOMETHING THAT'S OVER QUICKLY!
GO!
SUGAR, SUGAR--
--YOU ARE MY...
STOP!
I'VE HEARD ENOUGH!
I'LL LET YOU KNOW MY DECISION SOON!
BUT SOME ADVICE FOR YOU--
ME?
5

DROP THE CROWN, KID! THERE'S NO ROYAL FAMILY IN THIS COUNTRY!
YIKES! YOU DON'T MESS WITH "THE CROWN"!
SURE! I'LL DROP THE CROWN... WHEN YOU STOP WEARING THOSE TODDLER-SIZED T-SHIRTS!
HMPH!
GREAT, JUGHEAD! YOU JUST BLEW IT FOR US!!
SO WHAT? WE DON'T NEED THEM!
WATCH OUT FOR THESE CAMERAS!
WE BING
WHAT'S GOING ON?
JUGHEAD, ISN'T THAT YOUR COUSIN, BINGO?
IT'S HIS BAND, the BINGOES! LOOKS LIKE THEY'RE GOING TO PLAY!
HEY, JUGHEAD!
the Bingoes
6

WHAT'S WITH ALL THE CAMERAS?
IT'S PART OF OUR REALITY SHOW, "THAT WILKIN BOY"!
IT'S ABOUT OUR ROAD TO FAME AS A STRUGGLING ROCK BAND! WE'RE NOT AS FAMOUS AS The ARCHIES, YOU KNOW... YET!
WE BIN
MAYBE THAT'S WHAT WE NEED! A REALITY SHOW!
I DO HAVE A FACE FOR TV, YOU KNOW!
RING
TOO LATE FOR THAT!
WHY?
IT'S MARCY!! WE MADE IT! WE'RE ON The X FACTOR FINALE!
WOW! I THOUGHT WE BLEW IT!
SIMON MUST RESPECT A NO-NONSENSE GUY LIKE MYSELF!
YOU'RE ALL WELCOME, BY THE WAY!
7

LET'S CELEBRATE AT POP'S!
YOU'VE FINALLY SAID SOMETHING WORTHWHILE!
SOON, AT POP'S...
CONGRATS, GUYS!
SO IT LOOKS LIKE "The ARCHIES" ON X FACTOR...
...AND JOSIE AND THE PUSSYCATS ON AMERICAN IDOL!
WHAT?
LOOK!
ROCK BAND JOSIE AND THE PUSSYCATS HAVE BEEN SIGNED FOR THE FINALE OF AMERICAN IDOL!
POP TV
SIGH!
UH-OH! HE'S SPOTTED VALERIE!
AREN'T THE PUSSY-CATS OFF ON A EUROPEAN TOUR?

IT DOESN'T LOOK THAT WAY TO ME...
JOSIE! MELODY!
VALERIE!
ARCHIE!
WHEN DID YOU GET BACK?
YESTERDAY! I MEANT TO CALL YOU!
BUT WE RUSHED TO MEET WITH J. LO OVER AT "AMERICAN IDOL"!
SO WE HEARD!
WE'RE ON THE FINALE!
BUT CAN YOU BELIEVE SHE MADE US AUDITION?
RIVE
SAME HERE! FOR SIMON!
OF COURSE, SHE MADE THE OTHER ESTABLISHED ACTS AUDITION, LIKE CHRISTINA AGUILERA AND KATY PERRY!
9

SO, HOW'D WE SOUND, J.LO?
OKAY, I SUPPOSE!
BUT YOU DO SOUND A LITTLE RASPY, VALERIE!
SORRY, I DON'T USE AUTO-TUNE OR THIRTY ENGINEERS TO BOOST MY VOCAL RANGE!
ARE YOU INSINUATING THAT I DO?!
WELL, IF THE AUTO-TUNE FITS...
GIGGLE! THEY'VE GOT SPUNK, THAT'S FOR SURE! BOOK 'EM!
LET'S CELEBRATE ON OUR OWN...! BYE, GUYS!
CAN'T YOU EMBARK ON ANOTHER EUROPEAN TOUR?
THERE GOES OUR ARCHIE!
POP'S
10

PETE'S
PETE'S PETS
HEY, LOOK! IT'S ARCHIE AND VALERIE! THEY'RE FROM TWO FAMOUS ROCK GROUPS!
WE COULD GET A LOT OF ATTENTION IF WE GET THEM ON OUR REALITY SHOW!
NO PROBLEM! ARCHIE AND VALERIE! OVER HERE!!
HEY, BINGO! HAVE YOU MET VALERIE?
HEY!
HI!
DO YOU GUYS WANT TO WATCH US PERFORM?
SURE! WHY NOT?
LET'S DO A ROMANTIC BALLAD...
...FOR THE LOVEBIRDS!
The Bingoes
11

GET THEM ON CAMERA!!
SO!
I WISH ARCHIE WAS AROUND! WE NEED TO PRACTICE!
WELL, HE'S ALL OVER THE NEWS! HIM AND VALERIE, THAT IS! LOOK!
The Archies
TONIGHT ON "THAT WILKIN BOY," ARCHIE AND VALERIE DROP BY...
...AND THINGS ARE HEATING UP!!
12

THEY'RE GETTING MORE MEDIA BUZZ THAN US!
IT'S ALL GOOD! ALL MEDIA BUZZ IS GOOD!
ESPECIALLY FOR THE BINGOES! NOBODY HEARD OF THEM UNTIL THEY LATCHED ONTO ARCHIE AND VALERIE!
AND THE CAMERAS FOLLOW THEM EVERYWHERE...
CAMERAS HAVE BEEN FOLLOWING US EVERYWHERE!
I DON'T CARE!
AS LONG AS I'M WITH YOU!
DO YOU REALIZE WE'RE BEING CAST ASIDE ON OUR OWN SHOW?
THE RATINGS FOR THE SHOW HAVE QUAD-RUPLED!
IF YOU WANT TO STAY ON THE AIR, EMBRACE IT!
NOW, GO TO YOUR FRIENDS!
!
13

HI, GUYS!
OH, BINGO! SAMANTHA! TEDDY! HI, AGAIN.
WE'VE BEEN SEEING A LOT OF YOU!
YEAH, HOW ABOUT THAT?

SO...
THIS ARCHIE AND VALERIE SOAP OPERA IS REALLY PLAYING OUT!
AND WE'VE GOT HALF OF THE MAGIC COUPLE ON OUR FINALE!

WHAT?!
THEN BRING IT ON, J. LO!!
SLAM
BRING IT ON!
LOOK AT THIS! THEY'RE USING US AS BAIT FOR THE FINALES OF BOTH SHOWS!
IT'S THE BATTLE OF THE LOVEBIRDS IN THE FINALES OF THE YEAR!
WHO WILL YOU WATCH?!
WHO CARES?
LET'S GO TO POP'S!
15

Oh, NO! IT'S THOSE CAMERAS AGAIN!
LET'S RUN!
giggle! THIS IS FUNNY!
LET'S SEE IF WE CAN OUTRUN THEM!
YIKES! MORE CAMERAS!
OVER HERE!
UNDER THE BRIDGE!
WE DID IT! WE OUTRAN THEM!
YOU KNOW, IT'S KIND OF ROMANTIC UNDER HERE!
HERE! I HAVE A CANDY BAR WE CAN SHARE!
WHAT A ROMANTIC DINNER! AND IT'S QUIET HERE, ISN'T IT?
16

I LIKE IT!
SO DO I! BET I'LL GET SOME REAL MOOLAH FOR THIS!
SO...
KID, THIS IS GREAT!
THIS WILL BE GREAT FOOTAGE, FOR The BINGOES' FINALE!
SO!
IT'S THE BIG NIGHT! I HOPE YOU'VE BEEN PRACTICING!
WE HAVE BEEN! DON'T WE SOUND GREAT?
FACTO
the Archies
AND I SEE THAT YOU'VE DITCHED THAT CROWN!
Oh, YES...
BUT I BROUGHT THIS...
MY "DRESS CROWN," FOR SPECIAL OCCASIONS!
Oh, BROTHER!
17

AND AT THE COMPETITION...
OKAY, PUSSYCATS! STEP IT UP! WE NEED MORE ENERGY!
?!
CLAP CLAP
OR WHAT?
OR I'LL BUMP YOU FROM THE FINALE!
I DON'T THINK YOU'D DO THAT! YOUR WHOLE SHOW IS RIDING THIS ARCHIE & VALERIE WAVE!
YOU'D NEVER BE ABLE TO FACE THE NETWORK IF YOU DID THAT!
SO WE'RE SAFE!
CORRECT?
Josie AND THE PUSSYCATS
THAT WAS PRETTY SMART, MELODY!
SOMETIMES YOU SURPRISE ME!
ME TOO!
18

SO!
LADIES AND GENTLEMEN... The ARCHIES!
LET'S HEAR IT FOR JOSIE AND THE PUSSYCATS!!
LATER, ON X FACTOR!
AND NOW IT'S TIME TO PICK OUR WINNERS...
BUT FIRST...
HOW ARE YOU DOING, ARCHIE?
Oh, uh... FINE!
DO YOU MISS VALERIE?
Oh... I-- OF COURSE!
ISN'T THIS SUPPOSED TO BE OUR MOMENT?
YOU WOULDA THOUGHT...
AWWWWW!!
WE ♥ the ARCHIES
19

AND AT AMERICAN IDOL...
AND OUR WINNER WILL SOON BE DECIDED...
...BY VALERIE!
THAT'S RIGHT! HERE ARE THE FINAL TWO!
ME?!?
WHOEVER YOU PICK IS THE WINNER!
THAT'S CRAZY!
IT SURE IS!
ISN'T IT, SIMON COWELL?!!
THIS IS GETTING OUT OF HAND!
I'M NOT DOING THIS!
AND SOON...
AND THE WINNER IS...
KELLY CLARKSTOWN!!
...CLAY SMOKESTACK!
20

AND WE'LL LET THE ARCHIES PLAY US OUT!
AND CLAY, OUR WINNER... WILL SING A DUET WITH VALERIE!
??!?
WHAT?!
HIT IT!!
ISLANDS IN THE STREAM...
...I DON'T EVEN KNOW THIS SONG!
LATER IN THE EVENING...
WHAT?!
OUR RATINGS STUNK!!
AND SO DID J. LO'S! HOW COULD THIS BE?!
FROM THIS LAST MINUTE PROGRAM CHANGE!
21

The BINGOES PUT UP THEIR FINALE AGAINST US AT THE LAST MINUTE!
THEY TWITTERED AND FACEBOOKED ALL THEIR FANS!
WITH TEASERS OF THESE EXCLUSIVE SHOTS OF ARCHIE AND VALERIE!
"THAT WILKIN BOY" BEAT BOTH SHOWS!
SO... BINGO, CONGRATS ON YOUR REALITY SHOW GETTING RENEWED!
THANKS! WE'RE GETTING GIG REQUESTS, TOO!
ALL BECAUSE OF THOSE KILLER RATINGS FOR THE FINALE OF "THAT WILKIN BOY"!
WHAT'S EVEN MORE AMAZING IS...
...WE WEREN'T EVEN ON IT!!
BINGO!!
END

1

SEND IN THE CLOWNS!
2

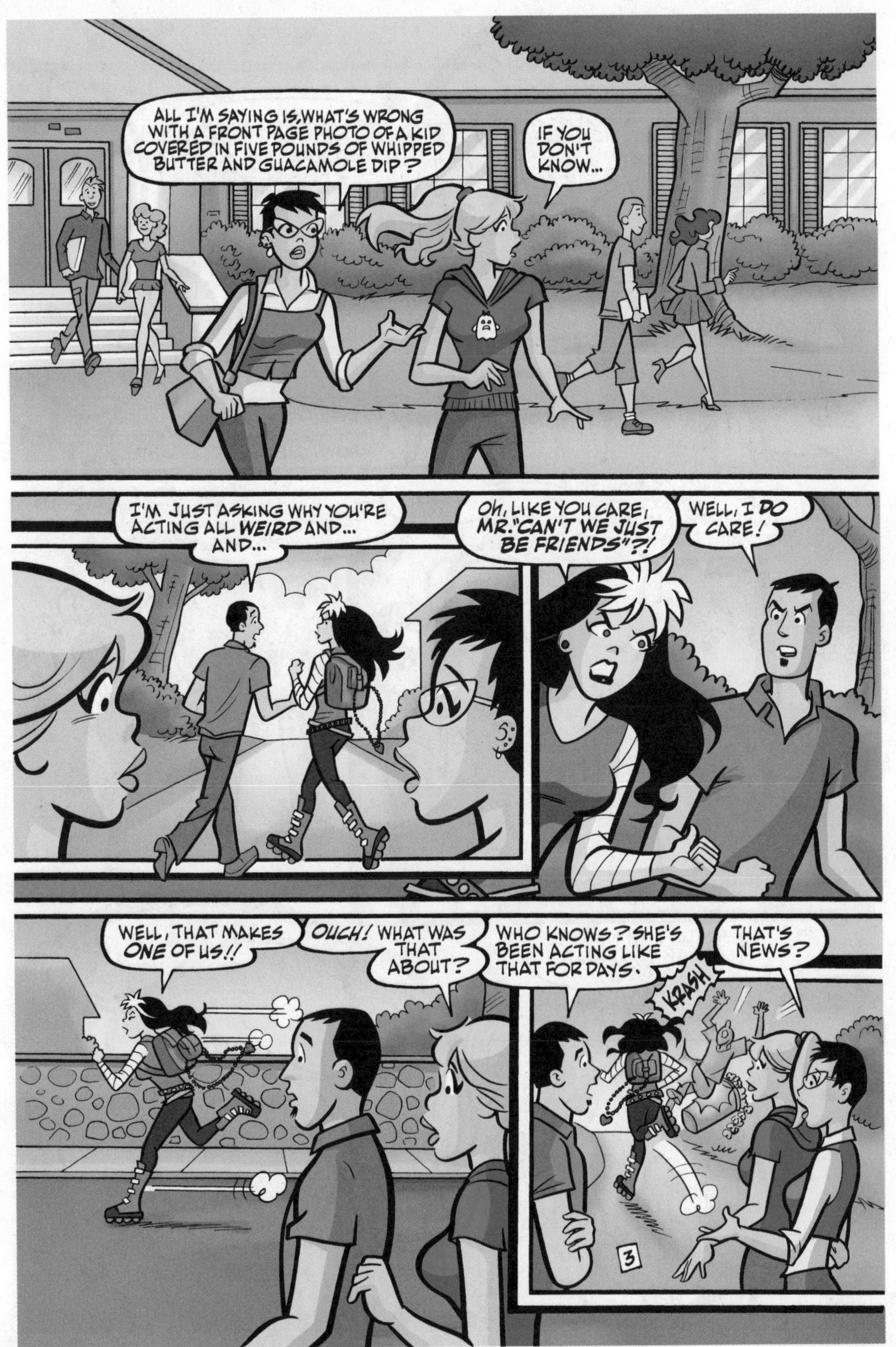
ALL I'M SAYING IS, WHAT'S WRONG WITH A FRONT PAGE PHOTO OF A KID COVERED IN FIVE POUNDS OF WHIPPED BUTTER AND GUACAMOLE DIP?
IF YOU DON'T KNOW...
I'M JUST ASKING WHY YOU'RE ACTING ALL WEIRD AND... AND...
OH, LIKE YOU CARE, MR. "CAN'T WE JUST BE FRIENDS"?!
WELL, I DO CARE!
WELL, THAT MAKES ONE OF US!!
OUCH! WHAT WAS THAT ABOUT?
WHO KNOWS? SHE'S BEEN ACTING LIKE THAT FOR DAYS.
KRASH
THAT'S NEWS?
3

WHAT? FACE IT, SAYID... SHRILL IS OUT THERE!
NOT MY FAULT YOU GO FOR THE WACKY ONES!
AVALON--uh... I MEAN SHRILL--CAN BE DIFFICULT, BUT NOT LIKE THIS. SOMETHING'S UP, AND SOMEONE NEEDS TO TALK TO HER TO FIND OUT WHAT!
I GUESS I COULD RUN SOME QUESTIONS BY HER, Y'KNOW, CHECK HER OUT AND...
NO, NO, NO! I DON'T WANT IT SPLATTERED ALL OVER SOME RIVER-DALE RAG!
HEY!
SORRY.
I JUST MEAN SOMEBODY SHOULD TALK TO HER... SOMEBODY WHO'S SENSITIVE, UNDERSTANDING AND NON-THREATENING!
WHO?
WELL, I THINK IT'S CLEAR HE DOESN'T MEAN ME!
oh.
4

HEY, SHRILL!
Oh, WOW. IT'S THE GOOD WITCH OF THE--
I COME IN PEACE.
THESE ARE SOME OF VIC'S BEST PUMPKIN WALNUT CUPCAKES...
I DON'T--
WITH VANILLA AND CARAMEL FROSTING...
WOW! MY FAVORITE!!
DON'T LET HER FOOL YOU! SHE SCARFS THESE DOWN LIKE ANYTHING!
KAYLEE!
IT'S TRUE! AND VIC KNOWS IT!
5

WHY ARE YOU HERE, BETTY?
WELL, PEOPLE ARE WORRIED ABOUT YOU.
YOU MEAN SAYID?
I MEAN PEOPLE. AND YES, HE'S ONE OF THEM.
HOW THOUGHTFUL.
THAT'S NOT WHAT SHE SAID WHEN THEY WERE GOING TOGETHER.
KAYLEE...
...DON'T YOU WANT MILK WITH THOSE THINGS?
Oh, YEAH!
I'LL GET SOME...
WHILE YOU TALK ABOUT YOUR EX-BOYFRIEND!
OOOOOO!
SHE'S CUTE!
LOOK, BETTY...
6

THERE'S NO POINT IN YOU DOING THIS WELCOME WAGON THING...
I'M JUST TRYING TO BE A FRIEND.
NO POINT IN THAT, EITHER. I WON'T BE AT RIVERDALE HIGH MUCH LONGER!
WHY? YOU'RE NOT IN ANY TROUBLE ARE YOU?
HEY, AVY! CAN I TAKE MY MEDS WITH MILK?
NO, ONLY CLEAR STUFF, LIKE WATER.
AND DON'T CALL ME THAT!
HERE, LET ME.
7
OH, NO!

NEXT DAY...
I REMEMBERED THE NAME OF THE MEDICATION FROM AN INTERNSHIP I DID AT THE HOSPITAL!
SO WHEN I ASKED, SHE TOLD ME KAYLEE NEEDS TREATMENT... FOR CANCER.
WOW! THAT'S TOUGH FOR AN ADULT! BUT A KID! DOUBLE WOW!
YES, HOSPITALS CAN BE SO COLD ...AND SCARY.
WELL... IT'LL BE A LITTLE DIFFERENT FOR KAYLEE.
SHE'S GOING TO RONALD McDONALD HOUSE IN NEW YORK CITY!
I'VE HEARD ABOUT IT!
KIDS AND TEENS STAY THERE WHILE GETTING TREATMENT! THAT'S GREAT!
ONLY PROBLEM IS... THE WHOLE FAMILY HAS TO MOVE THERE. SHRILL AND HER DAD.
THAT MEANS ANOTHER TRANSFER TO ANOTHER NEW SCHOOL. AND SHE'S JUST GETTING USED TO US!
SHRILL LOVES HER SISTER SO MUCH. SHE JUST WISHES SHE DIDN'T HAVE TO GO.
MAYBE WE CAN HELP SOMEHOW.
LET'S CALL THE REST OF THE GOODWILL GIRLS AND SEE IF WE CAN COME UP WITH SOME IDEAS!
8

THAT'S A GREAT IDEA! AND I COULD ASK ARCHIE AND JUGHEAD, TOO!
AND ME!
Oh, WELL... SURE. BUT--
BUT WHAT? DID YOU THINK I WOULDN'T WANT TO HELP?
Uh, NO... OF COURSE NOT... IT'S JUST THAT YOU USUALLY... DON'T HAVE TIME FOR GOODWILL GIRL THINGS.
MAYBE THIS IS DIFFERENT.
OR MAYBE I JUST HAVE SOME FREE TIME IN MY BUSY SOCIAL CALENDAR!
AND BETTY'S RIGHT. LET'S GET THE REST OF THE GANG IN ON THIS, TOO!
Oh, ARCHIE-KINS!
9

BOP
BONK
GOT IT!!
NICE TOSS, VIC!
SAYS YOU...
GUESS WE'LL TAKE CARE OF SHRILL...
JUST AS SOON AS WE TAKE CARE OF HIM!

NOK
NOK
NOK
GOODWILL GIRLS REPORTING FOR DUTY!
WOW!
WHAT'RE YOU ALL DOING HERE?!
STANDING IN THE DOORWAY, FOR THE MOMENT!
WHICH IS NOT GETTING THE JOB DONE, PEOPLE!
THERE'S NOTHING YOU CAN DO. WE HAVE TO--
MOVE. YES, I GOT THAT PART.
HI, MR. PRISSTON! I'M VERONICA LODGE! I BROUGHT MY PEOPLE TO HELP GET THIS THING ORGANIZED!
PLEASED TO MEET YOU!
11

OH, NOW WE'RE HER PEOPLE!
GEEZ! WHAT DO YOU GUYS THINK YOU CAN DO?
LOTS!
WE SPOKE TO PEOPLE IN YOUR COMMUNITY, AND TWO OF THEM VOLUNTEERED TO LOOK AFTER YOUR APARTMENT!
THAT'S VERY NICE, BUT WE CAN'T AFFORD THE RENT...
WE FOUND A COMMUNITY FUND THAT'LL COVER YOUR RENT FOR AT LEAST SIX MONTHS!
WHAT? BUT I NEVER...
WE KNOW YOU LEAVE IN A WEEK, SO WE'RE HERE TO HELP YOU PACK UP WHAT YOU NEED.
AND WHAT YOU MIGHT WANT TO STORE.
I'M NOT SURE WHAT TO TAKE! I HAVE SO MUCH--
OH, YOU DON'T HAVE TO PACK UP ANYTHING!
WHAT?
12

WE SPOKE TO CARLA, AND SHE SPOKE TO HER FOLKS, AND THEY DISCUSSED IT WITH--
CRIB NOTE VERSION, PLEASE.
YOU CAN STAY AT THEIR HOUSE. THEY HAVE PLENTY OF ROOM.
SO YOU DON'T HAVE TO LEAVE RIVERDALE HIGH IF YOU DON'T WANT TO!
BUT KAYLEE NEEDS ME.
WHO NEEDS WHO?
YOU'D BE LOST WITHOUT ME!
YES. I WOULD.
WELL, YOU GOTTA GROW UP SOMETIME. I'LL HAVE DAD... TO TAKE CARE OF.
BUT YOU'D BETTER CALL ME EVERY DAY.
YOU BET I WILL! TWICE A DAY!
NOW... SNIFFLE!
NOW THAT THAT'S SETTLED... SNIFFLE! LET'S GET TO WORK! WE HAVE...
13

"CLOTHING TO PACK FOR EVERYBODY. I'VE BEEN TO NEW YORK A THOUSAND TIMES, KAYLEE... SO I'LL HELP YOU PICK OUT SOME GREAT OUTFITS...
DVDS
BOOKS
"AND WE HAVE TO INSTRUCT YOUR APARTMENT SITTERS. BE SURE TO LEAVE SOME TREATS IN THE FRIDGE. THEY'LL LIKE THAT!
"MOOSE AND CHUCK CAN TAKE SHRILL'S THINGS OVER TO CARLA'S."
R
THREE DAYS LATER...
AND WITH ALL OF THAT DONE, WE CAN CONCENTRATE ON GETTING YOU TO NEW YORK!
OH, I RENTED A CAR SO WE CAN DRIVE THERE IN A FEW DAYS!
R
YES... YOU COULD DO THAT...
14

OR YOU COULD FLY THERE ON A JET, AND GET THERE IN A FEW HOURS!
Whoa!
MS. LODGE, I WRITE EDUCATIONAL MANUALS. IT'S A DECENT LIVING, BUT I CAN'T--
DADDY'S JET HAS A RUN TO NEW YORK ALREADY SCHEDULED FOR THIS WEEK. YOU COULD SIMPLY RIDE ALONG.
EVEN SHRILL COULD GO AND COME BACK ON THE SAME PLANE.
WHAT DO YOU THINK, KAYLEE?
A RIDE IN A JET? DO YOU REALLY HAVE TO ASK?
HOW CAN THIS BE?
IT'S WHAT WE CALL LIVING LODGE!
BUT I COULDN'T ASK SUCH A THING!
YOU DIDN'T. I OFFERED. NOW LET'S GET PACKIN', 'CAUSE--
"--NEXT STOP, RONALD McDONALD HOUSE IN NEW YORK CITY!"
15

RONALD McDONALD HOUSE
AND THIS WILL BE THE LIVING QUARTERS FOR YOU AND YOUR DAD, KAYLEE.
WHERE'S THE REST OF IT?
VERONICA!
I DIDN'T MEAN ANYTHING. I JUST THOUGHT THEY'D LIVE IN A FULL APARTMENT!
NINA
I KNOW WHAT YOU MEAN, VERONICA. WE'D LOVE TO OFFER MORE SPACE, BUT EVERY FAMILY RECEIVES THE SAME ACCOMODATIONS!
EVEN LARGER ONES?
YES. FAMILIES COME TO US FROM ALL OVER THE WORLD!
MANY HAVE TO GIVE UP EVERY-THING. WE WANT TO HELP AS MANY AS WE CAN!
16
NINA

WELL, THIS LOOKS GOOD TO ME!
I'M GLAD, BECAUSE WE HAVE A LOT MORE TO SHOW YOU, LIKE OUR ATRIUM.
AND THIS IS WHERE THE FAMILIES CAN PREPARE AND SHARE THEIR MEALS!
SO MANY CULTURES... SO MUCH FOOD... SO LITTLE TIME.
THEN THERE'S OUR COMPUTER LAB.
WHERE THEY'RE STUCK DOING HOME-WORK, JUST LIKE US!
ACTUALLY...
...THEY LEARN COMPUTER SKILLS, AND PUT OUT THEIR OWN NEWSPAPER!
THIS LOOKS LIKE FUN!
SOME CHILDREN RETURN FROM THEIR TREATMENTS AND COME DOWN HERE TO PLAY, DO ART PROJECTS, OR JUST RELAX.
ART, COMPUTERS, A TEEN ROOM, AND A GAME ROOM...
MAN, THE ONLY THING MISSING IS A MUSIC ROOM.
NO SOONER SAID--
17

--THAN DONE.
MANY OF THE OLDER KIDS LIKE THIS ROOM. A FEW HAVE EVEN FORMED BANDS -- AND PERFORMED FOR US!
THE PATIENTS?
NINA
THEIR SIBLINGS, TOO. REMEMBER, WHOLE FAMILIES LIVE WITH US.
SOMETIMES, A BROTHER OR SISTER NEEDS SOMETHING ELSE TO DO.
ALL OF THE THINGS YOU OFFER THE KIDS ARE AMAZING!
WE EVEN DO BLOCK PARTIES AND FUNDRAISERS TO HELP RAISE MONEY FOR SOME OF THIS!
I... I'M SORRY, BUT WE HAVE TO GO!
WE HAVE TO CATCH OUR RIDE BACK.
FEEL FREE TO COME BY ANY TIME YOU'RE IN TOWN.
WE CAN ALWAYS USE VOLUNTEERS!
I'LL SEE YOU UPSTAIRS.
18

OKAY, RONNIE...
WHEN ARE YOU GOING TO TELL ME?
TELL YOU WHAT?
WHAT'S BOTHERING YOU?
NOTHING. I--I--
WHEN I WAS LITTLE, I HAD AN UNCLE THOMAS. HE WAS MY MOTHER'S YOUNGEST BROTHER.
HE WAS NOT BUSINESS SAVVY, BUT HE WAS SO MUCH FUN. WE DID LOTS OF THINGS TOGETHER... HE COULD ALWAYS MAKE ME LAUGH, NO MATTER WHAT!
ONE DAY HE TOOK ME TO THE ZOO AND THE PARK. WE ATE TONS AND TONS OF ICE CREAM AND JUNK FOOD. THEN HE TOOK ME HOME... AND NEVER CAME TO VISIT AGAIN.
IT WAS A LONG TIME BEFORE THEY TOLD ME HE'D BECOME SICK... AND DIED.
CANCER?
I COULDN'T DO ANYTHING FOR UNCLE THOMAS, BUT I CAN FOR KAYLEE.
I JUST WISH I COULD DO MORE.
19

MAYBE YOU CAN. MAYBE WE ALL CAN.!
NINA SAID THEY ALWAYS HAVE TO RAISE MONEY TO SUPPORT THE GREAT THINGS THEY DO...
SO THE ARCHIES WILL DO A FUNDRAISER!
AND MAYBE YOUR DAD CAN CALL IN A FEW GUEST CELEBS TO HELP PACK THE HOUSE!
ESPECIALLY THOSE CELEBRITY CHEFS! YUM!
AND THE RONALD McDONALD HOUSE KIDS' BAND COULD JAM WITH US!
BUT WHERE COULD WE HAVE IT?
DON'T WORRY ABOUT THAT!
I'VE GOT A LOT MORE STRINGS TO PULL! WE'VE GOT A LOT TO DO...
"...IF WE'RE GOING TO PULL THIS TOGETHER!"
20

"SO LET'S GET TO IT!"
AND, OVER THE NEXT FEW MONTHS...
MADISON SQUARE GARDEN
TONIGHT
The Archies
I STILL CAN'T BELIEVE YOU GOT THIS PLACE FOR THE CONCERT!
THEY SUDDENLY HAD A DARK NIGHT AND WE HAD THE CASH...
...AND CELEBRITY CLOUT. ESPECIALLY WHEN I TOLD THEM WHAT IT WAS FOR.
THANK YOU FOR EVERYTHING...
...AUNT VERONICA!
ANYTIME, SWEETIE. ANYTIME.
21

I WISH I KNEW HOW TO THANK YOU.
ME, TOO! THIS IS MORE THAN...
DON'T TRY.
WE'RE ALL DOING THIS FOR THE RIGHT REASON.
THEN LET'S GET OUT THERE AND SHOW 'EM WHY WE'RE HERE!
HEY THERE, BIG C-- IT'S TIME YOU AN' ME REALIZE YOU CANNOT STAY--AND WENT OUR SEPARATE WAYS!
Ronald McDonald House
YEAH!
END

The Archies ROCKIN' WORLD TOUR PART ONE!
BOLLYWOOD LOVE!
I DID IT!! I'VE ALMOST SOLD MY FIRST DOCUMENTARY PITCH TO A MAJOR HOLLYWOOD STUDIO!
THAT'S GREAT, RAJ!
WHAT'S THE DOCUMENTARY ABOUT?
IT'S ABOUT YOU GUYS! The ARCHIES!
WHAT?! HOW'D WE GET INVOLVED IN THIS?
1

WELL, I SHOWED HIM ALL OF THE FOOTAGE I SHOT OF The ARCHIES SINCE I MOVED TO RIVERDALE!
THEY WANT TO DO A CONCERT FILM/ DOCUMENTARY OF YOUR UPCOMING TOUR!
WITH ME AS THE DIRECTOR!
WELL, ARCHIE! THIS IS OUR FIRST WORLD TOUR! WE KICK IT OFF IN MUMBAI, INDIA!
IT WOULD BE GOOD PROMOTION!
THIS IS TURNING OUT TO BE SOME TOUR!
YEAH! WE'VE GOT The BINGOS AND The MADHOUSE GLADS ON THE BILL, TOO!
WE'LL NEED OUR MANAGER TO WORK OUT THE LOGISTICS!
I'M ON IT!
HI MARCY!
2

SO...
Pinnacle PICTURES
ALL RIGHT! I THINK WE'RE HEADING IN THE RIGHT DIRECTION ON THIS!
WE JUST FEEL THE TOUR IS MISSING ONE THING!
WHAT'S THAT?
JOSIE AND THE PUSSYCATS!!
BUT THEY'RE HEADLINING THEIR OWN TOUR!
WE FEEL THERE'S A DYNAMIC BETWEEN The ARCHIES AND THE PUSSYCATS THAT IS IMPORTANT!
WE THINK WE NEED THAT TO "CLINCH" THIS DEAL!
AH, YOU MEAN THE ROMANCE BETWEEN ARCHIE AND VALERIE?
YOU COULD SAY THAT!
WHEN WE WATCHED RAJ'S FOOTAGE OF The ARCHIES, ONE THING RIVETED US...
3

THE DYNAMIC RELATIONSHIP BETWEEN VALERIE AND ARCHIE!
THERE'S ONE PROBLEM! ARCHIE AND VALERIE HAVEN'T SPOKEN IN MONTHS! THEY'RE ON THE OUTS!
WELL, SEE IF YOU CAN INTEREST THE PUSSYCATS IN JOINING YOU! THEN MAYBE SPARKS WILL FLY AGAIN!
SO...
NOW, MARCY...
WHY WOULD JOSIE AND THE PUSSYCATS TOUR WITH The ARCHIES? THEY'RE HEADLINERS!
WHAT IF THE PUSSYCATS AND The ARCHIES SHARED THE BILL?
WELL, WHAT'S IN IT FOR US?
A DOCUMENTARY MADE BY PINNACLE STUDIOS!
PINNACLE? WOW!
4

THAT WOULD BE A GREAT PROMOTION!
BUT ARCHIE AND VALERIE ARE ON THE OUTS! THEY MAY NOT WANT TO DO IT!
YEAH... WHAT CAN WE DO ABOUT THAT?
MEANWHILE...
Hmm-mm
Oh, HELLO, VALERIE!
HELLO, ARCHIE! FUNNY RUNNING INTO YOU HERE.
YEAH, WELL...
I HAVE JUST ONE THING TO SAY TO YOU...
PUCKER UP, RED!!

:GIGGLE!:
THIS IS SORT OF FUN, SNEAKING AROUND!
HEY, IT'S THE ONLY WAY TO KEEP THE PRESS AWAY! THEY ALMOST RUINED US WITH ALL THAT FOLLOWING US AROUND!
BY PRETENDING WE'RE NOT INVOLVED EVERYTHING IS SO MUCH EASIER!
YEAH, AND IT KEEPS BETTY AND VERONICA OFF MY BACK!
C'MON, LET'S GO HANG OUT IN MY GARAGE!
WE CAN WRITE SOME SONGS, TOO!
OR NOT.
6

SOON...
TOUR WITH The ARCHIES? FOR A DOCU-MENTARY TOO?
SOUNDS LIKE A GREAT OPPORTUNITY!
BUT WITH YOU AND ARCHIE NOT TALKING...
I SAY WE SHOULD DO IT! IT'S A GREAT OPPORTUNITY! ARCHIE AND I SHOULDN'T BE AN ISSUE...
AND...
THE PUSSYCATS HAVE AGREED TO JOIN THE TOUR!
BUT THERE IS THE ISSUE OF YOU AND VALERIE!
I'M A PROFESSIONAL! LET'S DO IT!
GREAT!
SO...
HA! WE GET TO TOUR TOGETHER!
DO YOU THINK WE SHOULD KEEP UP THIS CHARADE?
7

IF WE WANT THE PRESS OUT OF OUR BUSINESS, YES!
OKAY! IF JAY-Z AND BEYONCE HID THEIR ROMANCE FOR SO LONG, SO CAN WE!
SO...
OKAY, BINGOS! ARE YOU READY TO PLAY MUMBAI?
I CAN'T WAIT!
AND MADHOUSE GLADS! ARE YOU READY?
GATE 7
YOU BET!
WHERE ARE The ARCHIES?
THEY GET THEIR OWN PRIVATE JET! THEY ARE HEAD-LINERS, AFTER ALL!
WOW! MUST BE NICE!
The Archies
AS DO JOSIE AND THE PUSSYCATS!
OF COURSE!
Josie
8

SO...
WOW! IS MUMBAI REALLY INDIA'S BIGGEST CITY?
IT SURE IS!
Hotel Mumbai
IT FEELS GOOD TO BE BACK!
IT'S BEEN A WHILE SINCE I'VE BEEN HERE!
OH, LOOK! THE PUSSYCATS ARE HERE TOO!
HELLO, GIRLS!
ER... HELLO, ARCHIE.
HELLO, VALERIE.
Wink!
giggle!
YOU CAN CUT THE TENSION WITH A KNIFE!
9

I KNOW! ISN'T IT GREAT?!
LEAVES ROOM FOR ME AND ARCHIEKINS!
HE'S JUST AS MUCH MY ARCHIEKINS AS HE IS YOURS!
THE PAPARAZZI ARE EATING THIS UP!
WHILE VALERIE AND I WILL GO COMPLETELY UNNOTICED!
SO...
THE BINGOS SOUND GREAT!
The BINGOS
THE MUMBAI COLISEUM IS AMAZING!
NEXT UP ARE THE MADHOUSE GLADS!
AND The ARCHIES WON TONIGHT'S COIN TOSS-- SO THEY CLOSE THE SHOW!
10

HOORAY!
YAY!
BRAVO!
WOW! THIS IS THE BIGGEST AUDIENCE WE'VE EVER PLAYED FOR!
HEY, GANG! YOU KNOW MR. DRUMMEL!
THE HEAD OF OUR RECORD LABEL!
YOUR NEW CD IS REALLY TAKING OFF!
YOUR NEW SONG, "HOT FOR YOU... (CUZ UR COOL)" IS CHARTING HERE IN INDIA!

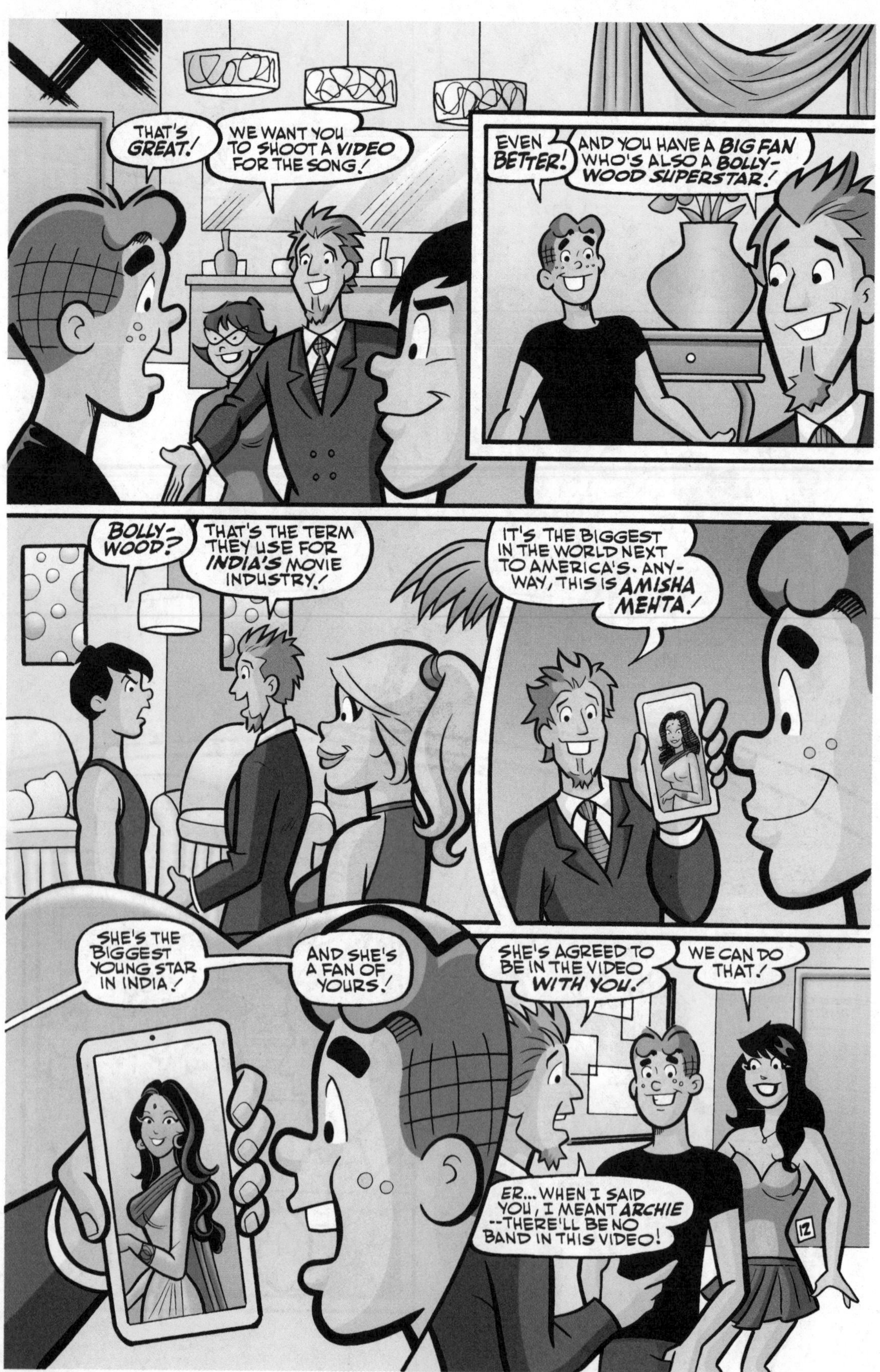
THAT'S GREAT!
WE WANT YOU TO SHOOT A VIDEO FOR THE SONG!
EVEN BETTER!
AND YOU HAVE A BIG FAN WHO'S ALSO A BOLLY-WOOD SUPERSTAR!
BOLLY-WOOD?
THAT'S THE TERM THEY USE FOR INDIA'S MOVIE INDUSTRY!
IT'S THE BIGGEST IN THE WORLD NEXT TO AMERICA'S. ANY-WAY, THIS IS AMISHA MEHTA!
SHE'S THE BIGGEST YOUNG STAR IN INDIA!
AND SHE'S A FAN OF YOURS!
SHE'S AGREED TO BE IN THE VIDEO WITH YOU!
WE CAN DO THAT!
ER... WHEN I SAID YOU, I MEANT ARCHIE --THERE'LL BE NO BAND IN THIS VIDEO!
12

THIS IS MORE OF A *CONCEPT* VIDEO!
WELL, WHO AM *I* TO ARGUE?
SOON!
HELLO, ARCHIE! I'M HONORED TO MEET YOU!
SAME HERE, AMISHA! YOU'RE *BEAUTIFUL*!
GAG ME WITH A SPOON!
IT'S SO EXCITING TO FILM THIS VIDEO ON THE STREETS OF MUMBAI WITH YOU!
THERE'S A LOT OF *DANCING* ON THESE STORY-BOARDS!
I DO A LOT DANCING IN MY FILMS!
LET'S START REHEARSING.
Hmph! WE GET VALERIE OUT OF THE PICTURE, AND *NEW* COMPETITION MOVES IN!
WE DON'T KNOW THAT! MAYBE SHE'S OKAY!
I DON'T KNOW...
13

LOOK AT THE WAY SHE LOOKS AT HIM!
HMM! WE BETTER KEEP AN EYE ON THEM!
:SIGH!:
WOW! THEY LIGHT UP THE SCREEN! EVEN DANCING THROUGH ALL THIS RAIN! IT NEVER RAINS LIKE THIS HERE!
I'VE NEVER SEEN ARCHIE DANCE LIKE THAT!
MAYBE YOU DON'T INSPIRE HIS DANCE MOVES!
SPLASH
IT'S STOPPED RAINING! LET'S GET THE CLOSE-UPS IN BEFORE IT RAINS AGAIN!
HMM... THAT AWNING LOOKS AWFULLY FULL OF WATER...
OH, REGGIE...

I'M ON IT!
I'M HAPPY TO RAIN ON ARCHIE'S HAPPY PARADE!
OH, MY LOVE...
YOU'RE SO HOT 'CUZ YOU'RE SO COOL!
DRIP
BLINK
SPLOOSH
MMM!!
SPTOOI!!
JUST KEEP ROLLING!
I LIKE IT!!
15

I'D LIKE TO KISS YOU!
WE DON'T KISS ON FILM HERE IN INDIA!
JUST LOOK INTO MY EYES.
THAT WORKS, TOO!
THAT'S A WRAP!
Oh, BROTHER! MORE COMPETITION!
AND THE PRESS GOES WILD...
MUMBAI REPORTER
IS IT TRUE LOVE for ARCHIE & AMISHA?!
The PULSE
IT'S Archie & Amisha!!
BOLLYWOOD ROMANCE
LOVE BIRDS HOLDING HANDS?
16

The Archies
The Archies
THIS IS MAKING FOR ONE EXCITING DOCUMENTARY!
AMISHA IS JOINING ARCHIE ONSTAGE!
THEY'RE GONNA SING TOGETHER!
I'M GONNA DIE!!
I KNOW THIS IS PROBABLY JUST FOR PUBLICITY...
The Arc
...BUT I HAVE TO FIND OUT IF ARCHIE REALLY LIKES HER!
17

SOON!
ARCHIE, DO YOU STILL LOVE ME? OR DO YOU HAVE FEELINGS FOR AMISHA?
VALERIE, I LIKE AMISHA...
gulp!
BUT I LOVE YOU!
THAT'S MY RED!
LATER...
I'LL HAVE TONS OF GREAT FOOTAGE FOR THE DOCUMENTARY!
WELL, I DON'T LIKE IT.
ARCHIE CARRYING ON WITH THIS AMISHA GIRL...
wha?!

CHERYL BLOSSOM?! WHAT ARE YOU DOING HERE? WITH ALEXANDRA CABOT OF ALL PEOPLE?!
I'M HERE TO OVERSEE THINGS!
THIS DOCUMENTARY IS GETTING OUT OF CONTROL!
WHAT DOES THIS HAVE TO TO DO WITH YOU?!
HAVEN'T YOU READ THE TRADES?
PINNACLE PICTURES WAS RECENTLY ACQUIRED...
HOLLYWOOD TIMES
...BY NONE OTHER THAN BLOSSOM ENTERPRISES!
WHAT?!
BLOSSOM ENTERPRISES ACQUIRES PINNACLE!
SO YOU BASICALLY WORK FOR ME!
19

SO CHERYL BLOSSOM IS RUNNING THIS SHOW NOW!
WITH THE HELP OF MY NEW BFF-- ALEXANDRA CABOT!
ANY QUESTIONS?
NEXT UP
The TOUR CONTINUES-- IN CHINA!
AND WITH MORE SURPRISES!
SURPRISES LIKE SPECIAL GUEST STAR--
Sabrina
THE TEENAGE WITCH
End

"Love on the Road"
The ARCHIE'S ROCKIN' WORLD TOUR!
PART 2
BUT HERE'S A RE-CAP OF LAST ISSUE!
THE ARCHIES, THE PUSSYCATS, THE BINGOS, AND THE MAD-HOUSE GLADS HAVE EMBARKED ON A WORLD TOUR STARTING IN INDIA!
IT'S BEING DOCU-MENTED BY RAJ PATEL FOR THE MAJOR STUDIO PINNACLE FILMS!
The Archies
The Archies
ARCHIE AND VALERIE HAVE REKINDLED THEIR ROMANCE (ALBEIT, IN PRIVATE).
BUT ARCHIE HAS BEEN PAIRED WITH BOLLYWOOD SUPERSTAR AMISHA MEHTA--AND THERE'S DEFINITELY A CONNECTION!
AND SUDDENLY, PINNACLE STUDIOS HAS BEEN PURCHASED BY BLOSSOM ENTERPRISES, AS IN CHERYL BLOSSOM!
HOW WILL THIS EFFECT THE DOCUMENTARY? AND THE TOUR? FIND OUT AS THE TOUR ARRIVES IN CHINA!
CHINA
1

I'VE NEVER BEEN TO SHANGHAI!
IT'S CHINA'S BIGGEST CITY!
WE HAVE A CONCERT THERE! BUT WAIT UNTIL WE GET TO BEIJING!
WHAT'S GOING ON THERE?
OUR BIGGEST CONCERT! IN FRONT OF THE GREAT WALL OF CHINA!
WHAT'S SO GREAT ABOUT IT?
ARE YOU KIDDING?
IT'S THE LARGEST FREE STANDING FORMATION IN THE WORLD! IT'S OVER 13,000 MILES LONG!
I'M NOT SO SURE ABOUT THIS!
I THINK THE GOBI DESERT IS A BETTER BACKDROP!

WHY IS SHE HERE?
WITH THAT TROUBLEMAKER ON HER SIDE?
I OWN PINNACLE STUDIOS NOW! SO I OWN THIS DOCUMENTARY!
TREAD CAREFULLY, CHERYL!
THIS DOCUMENTARY CAPTURES EVERYTHING... INCLUDING MANIACAL DIVAS WHO THINK THEY CAN CONTROL EVERYTHING!
BESIDES, I'M UPLOADING LITTLE SNEAK PEEKS DAILY! YOU WOULDN'T WANT TO LOOK BAD, WOULD YOU?
UH, WELL... NO...
AND YOUR DADDY OWNS THE STUDIO! YOU WOULDN'T WANT HIM TO GET MAD AT YOU, WOULD YOU?
ER...UH, WELL...
OKAY! I SEE WHERE YOU'RE GOING...
3

BUT BE CAREFUL! BECAUSE I'M STILL HERE WATCHING WHAT'S GOING ON!
PSSST! CHERYL!
I THOUGHT YOU SAID WE'D BE ABLE TO JOIN THE PUSSYCATS WITH YOUR NEW-FOUND POWER!
WE WILL! WE'LL FIGURE OUT A WAY!
BESIDES, I'LL HAVE PLENTY OF TIME TO PLAN...
I WON'T BE GETTING ANYWHERE WITH ARCHIE... HE'S SO BUSY WITH THAT AMISHA!
WHY IS SHE TRAVELING TO CHINA WITH US?
THE RECORD COMPANY LIKES HER!
Hmmm... WHERE'S THAT MUSIC COMING FROM...?
4

BETTY? ARE YOU PLANNING A SOLO ACT?
LET'S JUST SAY THE TAMBOURINE HAS ITS LIMITS!
OH, AND LOOK! YOU'RE SKYPING WITH GINGER, MIDGE, TONI AND SABRINA!
WE'RE JUST DOING A LITTLE CHICK ROCK 'N' ROLL THING!
COOL! CAN I GET IT ON TAPE?!
NOT QUITE YET! I DON'T THINK WE'RE READY!
WELL, MOST OF YOU ARE READY!
I'M STILL A LITTLE SHAKY ON KEYBOARD!
YOU'RE DOING JUST GREAT, SABRINA!
SABRINA! WHY DON'T YOU USE YOUR MAGIC AND OUTPLAY EVERYONE?
THE FUN PART IS LEARNING! I WANT TO BE A SKILLED MUSICIAN!
5

WELL, GOOD LUCK, BETTY!
:SIGH: IT'S NOT LIKE I HAVE ANY ROMANCE TO KEEP ME BUSY!
I WISH TREV* WAS ON THE PLANE WITH ME!
*TREV IS VALERIE'S BROTHER. BETTY AND TREV DATED BACK IN ARCHIE: A ROCK 'N' ROLL ROMANCE.
SO...
WOW! SHANGHAI IS BEAUTIFUL!
WE'LL BE PLAYING THAT ARENA OVER THERE!
I WISH WE WERE HEAD-LINING!
6

SOMEDAY, SAMANTHA! The ARCHIES ARE SO LUCKY.!
I WISH I HAD ARCHIE'S LUCK WITH THE LADIES!
HE AND VALERIE ARE QUITE THE TICKET.!
DON'T YOU MEAN WERE THE TICKET? THEY'RE NOT TOGETHER ANY-MORE!
OH, YES THEY ARE!
WELL, WILL YOU LOOK AT THAT.!
THAT REMINDS ME, I SAW SOME INTERESTING FOOTAGE OF ARCHIE AND AMISHA...
SO...
RUN THAT BY ME AGAIN, RAJ...
I WANT TO KISS YOU...
AGAIN...
I WANT TO KISS YOU...
7

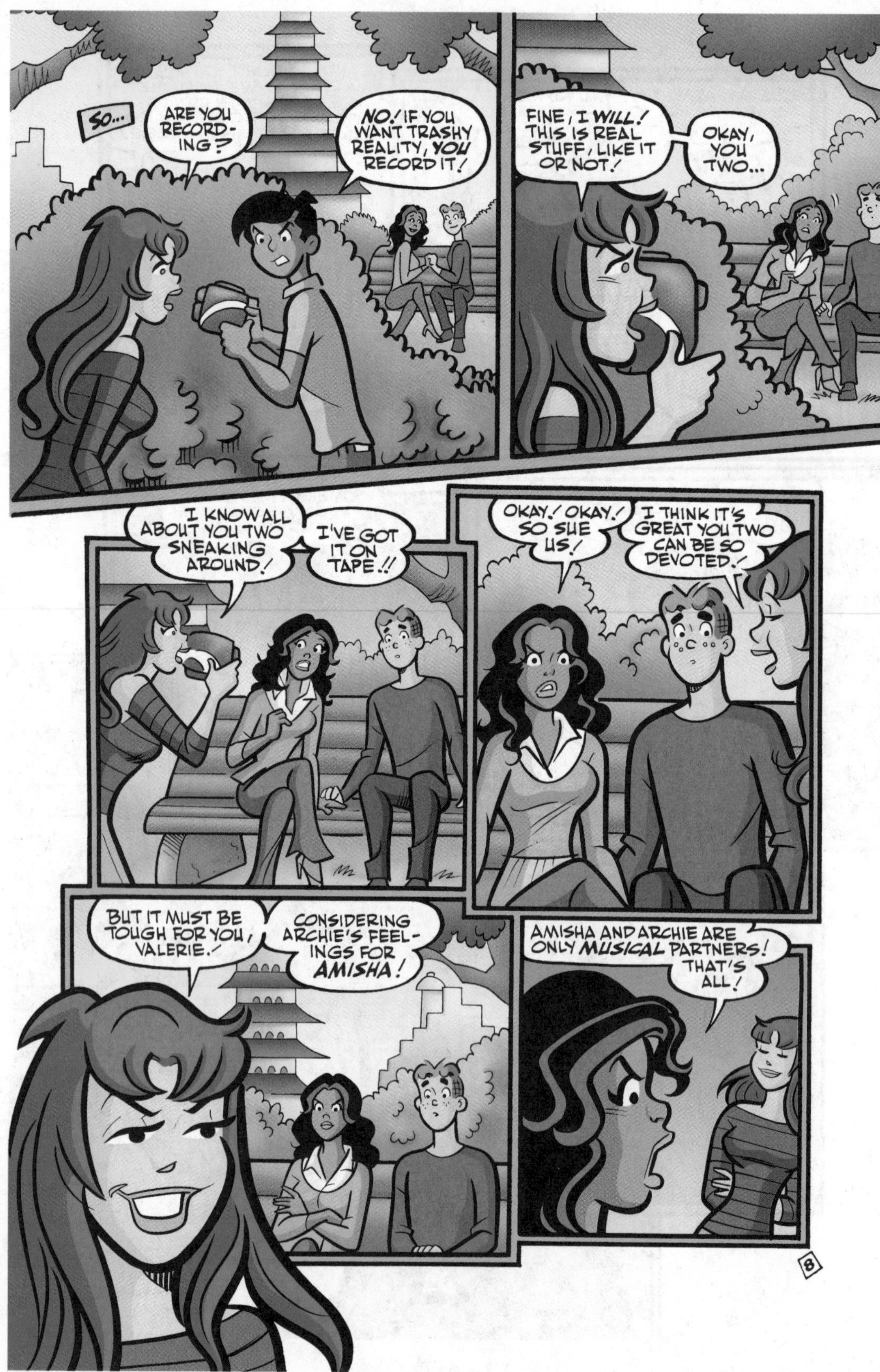
SO...
ARE YOU RECORD-ING?
NO! IF YOU WANT TRASHY REALITY, YOU RECORD IT!
FINE, I WILL! THIS IS REAL STUFF, LIKE IT OR NOT!
OKAY, YOU TWO...
I KNOW ALL ABOUT YOU TWO SNEAKING AROUND!
I'VE GOT IT ON TAPE!!
OKAY! OKAY! SO SUE US!
I THINK IT'S GREAT YOU TWO CAN BE SO DEVOTED!
BUT IT MUST BE TOUGH FOR YOU, VALERIE!
CONSIDERING ARCHIE'S FEEL-INGS FOR AMISHA!
AMISHA AND ARCHIE ARE ONLY MUSICAL PARTNERS! THAT'S ALL!
8

OH, REALLY? WATCH THIS, VALERIE!
I WANT TO KISS YOU...*
WE DON'T KISS ON FILM HERE...
*SEE LAST CHAPTER!
YOU WANTED TO KISS HER?
THAT LOOKED PRETTY REAL, ARCHIE!
I... I WAS JUST CAUGHT UP IN THE MOMENT!
WHEN WILL I LEARN?
I'M JUST ONE IN YOUR HAREM OF GIRLS THAT YOU GO THROUGH. WELL, YOU CAN REMOVE ME FROM YOUR ROTATION!
VALERIE! PLEASE!!
THANKS A LOT, CHERYL!
9

WHAT DID THAT ACCOMPLISH, CHERYL?
ARE YOU KIDDING?! SOMEONE MIGHT ACTUALLY WATCH THIS DOCUMENTARY NOW!
SO...
OH, ARCHIE! YOU POOR THING! YOU AND VALERIE BELONG TOGETHER!
BUT YOU AND I HAVE TO GO ON SOON!
CHEER UP!
SO...
PUSSYCATS! YOU WERE GREAT!
YEAH!
YOU WERE GREAT, VALERIE!
BREAK YOUR HEAD!
DON'T YOU MEAN LEG?
YOU HEARD ME!!
10

YOU'RE ON!
GO!
ARCHIE'S MIND IS ELSE-WHERE!
I THINK IT'S MORE VALERIE STUFF!
SIGH I REMEMBER WHEN HE USED TO GET WORKED UP OVER US!
SOON!
AND NOW A DUET WITH THE COUPLE OF THE YEAR... ARCHIE & AMISHA!
The Archies
AS MUCH AS I LOVE SINGING WITH ARCHIE...
HE SHOULD BE PERFORMING WITH THE ONE THAT HE REALLY LOVES...

...VALERIE SMITH!
GET OUT HERE!
HUH?
GO ON, VALERIE! THEY'RE CALLING FOR YOU!
UH, ER-- UH--
GO ON!!
YAY!!
THAT WAS NICE OF YOU, AMISHA!
WELL, IT'S JUST THAT ARCHIE IS SUCH A NICE GUY!
WE THOUGHT YOU TWO WERE GOING TO BE A COUPLE!
SIGH
SO DID I!
12

Oh, BABY, MY WORDS ARE TRUE...
BUT MY HEART IS BLUE
BEAUTIFUL!
I GUESS THEY'RE BACK TOGETHER!
WOO!!
THAT WAS GREAT!
ENCORE!
I LOVE YOU, VALERIE.
VALERIE...?
WE'RE NOT BACK TOGETHER!
AND I WON'T BE COERCED OR PRESSURED BY ONE SONG TO-GETHER!
OKAY, GLADS! YOU'RE ON!
13

THE NEXT DAY...
WE'RE OFF TO BEIJING! YAY!
WE GUYS WILL MEET UP WITH YOU ON THE NEXT PLANE!
A BLOG WANTS TO DO A FASHION SPREAD ON US GUYS!
OKAY! THE REST OF US WILL SEE YOU THERE!
SO...
THE GREAT WALL OF CHINA!! THERE AREN'T MANY CONCERT EVENTS ALLOWED HERE!
THIS WILL BE THE OPPORTUNITY OF A LIFETIME!
14

WE SHOULD PROBABLY START PRE-PARING!
ARCHIE'S FLIGHT SHOULD BE ARRIVING SOON!
DON'T COUNT ON IT!
THE AIRPORT IN SHANGHAI IS SHUT DOWN!
WHAT?!
THERE'S A TROPICAL STORM! THE PLACE IS SHUT DOWN!
YOU'LL HAVE TO GO ON WITHOUT HIM!
WE ONLY HAVE 2/5 OF The ARCHIES HERE!
HOW DO WE HEAD-LINE WITH THAT?
THE BETTYS! IT'LL BE YOUR WORLD DEBUT!
WHAT?!
15

ISN'T THAT THE NAME OF YOUR BAND?!
YES! THE BETTYS!
BUT THE GIRLS ARE BACK IN RIVER-DALE!
NO, WE'RE NOT!
WHA--?! H-HOW--?! WHE--?!
I DON'T KNOW HOW WE GOT HERE EITHER!
?!?
I COULDN'T HELP IT!
WHEN I SAW ON ARCHIE'S FACEBOOK PAGE THAT THEY WERE STRANDED...
I HAD TO POP US OVER HERE TO SAVE THE DAY!
WHY DIDN'T YOU JUST USE YOUR MAGIC TO ZAP The ARCHIES HERE?
Oh, WELL! I GUESS I DIDN'T THINK OF THAT.
YEAH, RIGHT! YOU JUST WANT THE SPOT-LIGHT!

DO YOU FEEL READY TO GO ON?
WOW! OUR ALL-GIRL BAND PLAYING THE GREAT WALL!!
LET'S SHOW THEM THE MEANING OF GIRL POWER!!
TONIGHT! THE WORLD MEETS THE BETTYS!!
HOW EXCITING! LET'S GET ALL OF THIS ON TAPE!
NO PRESSURE, THOUGH! ONLY HALF THE WORLD WILL SEE IT!
GULP
17

WOW!
I DIDN'T KNOW THAT BETTY COULD ROCK LIKE THAT!
SHE'S GOT A LOT OF PENT UP ENERGY!
I'M KINDA JEALOUS!
AND PROUD!
The Bettys ARE SMOKING HOT!
The Bettys
YOU SEE THEM, ARCH?
YEAH! THEY SOUND GREAT!
THEY'RE GOING TO OUTSHINE The ARCHIES!
18

WELL, LET'S NOT GO THAT FAR!
MUST BE NICE TO BE PART OF ALL THAT EXCITEMENT!
SHE'S RIGHT!
THIS IS SUCH A MAGICAL MOMENT!
WE SHOULD ALL BE HERE TO ENJOY IT!
JOSIE and the PUSSYCATS
WE SHOULD ALL BE HERE!
WHAT?!
HOW?!
Huh?!
ZAP
HOW DID WE GET HERE?!
19

NEVER MIND! LET'S JUST ENJOY THE MOMENT!
LOOK AT THOSE FIREWORKS!
YEAH-- THERE'S FIRE-WORKS ALL RIGHT!
NEXT: THE TOUR CONTINUES IN-- Australia WITH KATY KEENE AND OTHER GUEST STARS!
?
?

ARCHIE'S ROCKIN' WORLD TOUR PART 3--
BLUNDER DOWN UNDER!
HI! I'M AMISHA! I'M GOING TO GIVE YOU THE RUN-DOWN ON WHAT HAPPENED IN THE LAST ISSUE!
"The ARCHIES WORLD TOUR CONTINUED INTO CHINA!
CHINA
"RAJ CONTINUED TO DOCUMENT THE CONCERT-- AS WELL AS ARCHIE AND VALERIE'S BREAK-UP...
"...WHICH WAS INSTIGATED BY NONE OTHER THAN CHERYL BLOSSOM AND HER COHORT ALEXANDRA CABOT!
R
"WHEN THE BANDS COULDN'T MAKE THEIR CONCERT AT THE GREAT WALL, BETTY'S GIRL BAND, The BETTYS PERFORMED TO GREAT ACCLAIM!"
NOBODY CAN FIGURE OUT HOW THEY GOT THERE... BUT NONE-THELESS, IT WAS A GREAT SUCCESS!
I HAD SOMETHING TO DO WITH IT!
The Betty's

I CAN'T BELIEVE WE'RE IN SUNNY AUSTRALIA!
SYDNEY IS SO BEAUTIFUL!
I CAN'T BELIEVE WE'RE GOING TO PLAY THE HISTORIC SYDNEY OPERA HOUSE!
YOU'RE GOING TO PLAY IN THE "ROCK 'N' ROLL FASHION-PALOOZA"!
IT'S A BENEFIT, WHERE OUR BANDS WILL PLAY, AS FAMOUS MODELS DISPLAY CLOTHES FOR CHARITY!
DID YOU HEAR THAT, ARCHIE? FASHION MODELS!
2

HE'S STILL BUMMED OUT OVER VALERIE!
C'MON, ARCH!
LIGHTEN UP!
WE'RE IN AUSTRALIA FOR TWO WEEKS!
ENJOY THE SITES OF THIS BEAUTIFUL PLACE!
I WILL!
THERE'S ONE BEAUTIFUL SITE RIGHT NOW!
SO...
I WANNA HOLD YOU 'TIL THE END OF TIME...
OOH! WHAT A BEAUTIFUL SONG!
IT DOES SOUND NICE! AND FAMILIAR!
3

I KNOW! THAT VOICE DOES SOUND FAMILIAR, DOESN'T IT?
C'MON, ARCHIE! WE'RE OFF TO SEE THE GOLD COAST!
MIND IF I JOIN YOU?
HEY! YOU'RE...
KATY KEENE!
THAT'S RIGHT!
I'M ORGANIZING THE ROCK N' ROLL FASHION PALOOZA!
I THOUGHT WE COULD GO OVER THINGS WHILE SIGHT-SEEING!
SURE THING!
RAJ! SHOULDN'T YOU BE FILMING THIS?
HAHA! I THINK RAJ IS ENAMORED WITH KATY!
4

SO...
THE GOLD COAST IS BEAUTIFUL!
IT SURE IS!
I'M GLAD ARCHIE CAME!
I THINK HE'S GOTTEN HIS MIND OFF OF YOU-KNOW-WHO!
SIGH!
MEAN-WHILE...
SO THIS IS ROYAL NATIONAL PARK!
ROYAL NATIONAL PARK

GASP!
THERE'S A KID NAMED JOEY IN THAT KANGAROO'S POUCH?!
NO, MELODY! JOEY IS A NAME FOR A BABY KANGAROO!
Oh, LOOK AT THAT KOALA!
HAVE YOU EVER SEEN SUCH AN ADORABLE FACE?
HE IS CUTE!
KINDA REMINDS ME OF SOMEONE...
SO, The BINGOS AND The MADHOUSE GLADS HIT MELBOURNE...
WOW! IT TOOK ONLY THREE HOURS ON THE BULLET TRAIN TO GET TO MELBOURNE...
6

WHY DIDN'T WE HANG AROUND SYDNEY LONGER?
I FEEL LIKE A THIRD WHEEL AROUND The ARCHIES AND The PUSSYCATS!
I KNOW! AND WE'RE THE FOURTH WHEEL!
BESIDES, "The DAMAGED GOODS" ARE ON TOUR, AND I WANT TO SEE THEIR SHOW HERE!
NOW PLAYING! The DAMAGED GOODS!
THE SHOW'S BEEN CANCELLED! THE BAND BROKE UP!
ARE YOU SURE?
I SHOULD KNOW! I'M THEIR MANAGER! WANT TO FILL IN FOR THEM?
YOU KNOW WHO WE ARE?!
OF COURSE! YOU'RE MY FAVORITE PART OF THE ROCKIN' WORLD TOUR!
7

REALLY? WOW! NICE TO BE NOTICED!
WE'LL DO IT!
SHOULDN'T WE CHECK IN WITH THE OTHERS?
THIS WON'T INTERFERE WITH OUR TOUR!
BESIDES! IT'S TIME FOR THE BINGOS AND THE GLADS TO TAKE CENTER STAGE!
HERE, HERE!
YOU'RE ON IN TWO HOURS!

THERE'S THAT SONG AGAIN!
Ah, YES! SHE'LL BE PART OF THE FASHION EVENT, TOO!
OF COURSE, YOU ALL GO BACK TOGETHER, DON'T YOU?
??
THAT VOICE! I JUST FIGURED OUT WHO IT IS!
THEN TELL ME!
IT'S OUR OLD PAL...
LATER...
BRIGITTE REILLY!!
YAY! IT'S BEEN SO LONG!!
WE'VE MISSED YOU SINCE YOU GRADUATED EARLY FROM RHS!
WELL, I WANTED TO FOCUS ON MY MUSIC!

WE HEAR YOUR SONG EVERY-WHERE!
I KNOW! IT'S A HIT HERE DOWN UNDER!
IT'S GOING TO BE RELEASED IN THE STATES NEXT MONTH!
I'M SO NERVOUS!
SHE'S SO MODEST!
LOOK! SHE'S ON THE COVER OF THIS AUSSIE MAGAZINE!
"BRIGITTE!"
WOW! YOU KNOW YOU'VE MADE IT WHEN YOU GO BY ONE NAME!!
AUSSIE MUSIC
Brigitte
SO, YOU TWO ARE STILL BATTLING IT OUT FOR ARCHIE?
THAT'S COMPLICATED!
IT ALWAYS WAS!
WE'LL FILL YOU IN...
10

THE NEXT DAY...
THE BINGOS AND THE GLADS GOT A GREAT REVIEW AT THEIR SHOW LAST NIGHT!
BINGOS ROCK THE HOUSE
I DIDN'T KNOW THEY WERE PER-FORMING!
NEITHER DID I...
SO...
WE'VE BEEN OFFERED THE REST OF "THE DAMAGED GOODS" DATES HERE IN AUSTRALIA!
WE CAN STILL PERFORM ON OUR TOUR! BUT WE REALLY WANT TO DO THIS!
WELL, I SUPPOSE!! JUST TELL US UP FRONT NEXT TIME!
YOU GOT IT!
WE'RE PERFORMING IN TOWN TONIGHT...

WOW! THEY ARE REALLY GOOD!
THEY'VE REALLY HIT THEIR STRIDE!
I'M GLAD WE LET THEM DO THEIR OWN THING!
HI, VALERIE!
HI, ARCHIE!
HEY, KIDS! WHAT'S UP?!
WHAT A PAIN THAT CHERYL IS!
12

AND ALEXANDRA'S NOT MUCH BETTER!
WE'VE GOT TO GET ARCHIE AND VALERIE ALONE TO PATCH THINGS UP.!
THINK! THINK! I KNOW.!
THERE'S A LITTLE DINGY TOUR RIGHT OUT OF MELBOURNE!
I'VE BEEN CALLED A LITTLE DINGY BEFORE!
WHAT A SHOCK!
ANYWAY, IF WE CAN GET THEM ALONE...
LATER...
GUYS! IT'S TWO DAYS UNTIL THE SHOW.!
YOU ALL HAVE TO BE FITTED FOR YOUR OUTFITS.!
13

YAY! SOMEONE'S SPEAKING MY LANGUAGE!
THE LANGUAGE OF VAPID!
I HAVE SOMETHING BLACK AND BLUE FOR YOU TO WEAR!
SO...
WOW! YOU ALL LOOK GREAT!!
PUSSYCATS WALK ON THE RUNWAY WITH THE GLADS IN TEN!
14

BRIGITTE! YOU'RE UP NEXT!
GORGEOUS!
The ARCHIES ARE GOING TO PLAY NOW!
WE'RE ALL HERE!
WHERE'S ARCHIE?!
I-- I CAN'T MOVE! THESE PANTS ARE TOO TIGHT!
THAT'S WHAT HAPPENS WHEN YOU DON'T COME TO THE FITTING!
AND THESE BOOTS ARE TOO HIGH!
NO TIME TO CHANGE! YOU'RE ON!!
OMIGOSH! HE'S WADDLING LIKE A DUCK!
C'MON!
15

WE'LL CARRY HIM OUT!
MEN ARE SUCH DOLTS SOMETIMES!
SO...
THAT WAS OKAY! AS LONG AS I DON'T HAVE TO MOVE, I'M FINE!
OKAY, GUYS! HIT THE RUNWAY WHILE THE PUSSYCATS PLAY!
WHAT?! I CAN'T GO ON ANY RUNWAY LIKE THIS!
IN THE NAME OF FASHION, DON'T MESS THIS UP!
ARCHIE! GO!!
OMIGOSH! HE'S HOPPING LIKE AN IDIOT!
THAT'S OUR ARCHIE!
HA! HA! HA!
CLOP CLOP CLOP
16

WELL, HE IS ENTERTAINING THE CROWD!
Whoops!
R-R-RIIIP!
YIKES! POOR ARCHIE!!
THEY'LL SEE YOUR UNDER-WEAR!!
B-BUT--
--I'M NOT WEARING ANY! I COULDN'T GET THESE PANTS ON OVER THEM!
HERE, RED!
COVER YOURSELF UP FOR CRYING OUT LOUD!
YOU CALLED ME RED!
DON'T GET ALL MUSHY! I JUST DIDN'T WANT TO SEE YOU HUMILIATED!
17

AWWW... ISN'T THAT SWEET!
WE HAVE A SPECIAL TREAT!
BRIGITTE WANTS TO PERFORM HER HIT "END OF TIME"!
YAY! WOO-HOO!!
I'M DEDICATING THIS TO ARCHIE AND VALERIE!
I'VE BEEN MISSING YOUR TOUCH...
GREAT! A BALLAD BY BRIGITTE! ARCHIE AND VALERIE ARE AS GOOD AS GOLD!
...I WANNA HOLD YOU 'TIL THE END OF TIME...
WE STILL HAVE TO TALK!
THAT'S GOOD ENOUGH FOR ME!
I WISH I HAD SOME-ONE TO HOLD!
18

HI, BABY!
OH, COME HERE!
HI, TREVOR!
HI, BETTY!
HELLO, TRIPLE DECKER BURGER!
SO...
AUSTRALIA WAS GRAND!
IT WAS EVEN BETTER SEEING BRIGITTE AGAIN!
WE RAISED SO MUCH MONEY FOR CHARITY!
THANKS TO ALL OF YOU!
HEY, WHERE ARE ARCHIE AND VALERIE?
19

WELL, WE HAD SET UP A LITTLE DINGY FOR THEM!
ARE YOU TALKING ABOUT MELODY?
THAT JOKE'S BEEN USED, DOLT!
I HOPE THEY'RE TALKING IT OUT!
"I HOPE SO!"
NEXT:
The WORLD TOUR WINDS UP IN CANADA!
End

ARCHIE'S ROCKIN' WORLD TOUR
PART 4
"CLOSE to the BORDERLINE"
KATY KEENE HERE! GIVING YOU A RE-CAP OF LAST ISSUE!
"THE ARCHIES AND THE OTHER BANDS CAME TO AUSTRALIA FOR THEIR TOUR... AND MY ROCK N' ROLL FASHION SHOW!
AUSTRALIA
"ARCHIE AND VALERIE WERE STILL ON SHAKY GROUND...
"...WHILE THE BINGOS AND THE GLADS HAD BRANCHED OUT ON THEIR OWN!
"OLD FRIEND BRIGITTE REILLY RETURNED!
"AND A NEW FRIEND AMISHA SORT OF WATCHED ON THE SIDELINES. I THINK SHE LIKES A CERTAIN REDHEAD!
"BUT THE BANDS MADE THEIR FANS HAPPY IN AUSTRALIA!
"AND ARCHIE AND VALERIE FOUND PEACE WITH EACH OTHER..."
...AND NOW FOR THE TOUR'S GRAND FINALE IN CANADA!

WE'RE HERE IN VANCOUVER! OUR FIRST STOP!
IT SEEMS WEIRD TO BE HERE WITHOUT THE BINGOS AND THE GLADS!
THEY'LL BE HERE FOR OUR FINAL SHOW IN TORONTO!
THEY'RE HAVING ALL KINDS OF SUCCESS DOWN UNDER IN AUSTRALIA!
WE CAN'T BEGRUDGE THEM THAT!
SURE WE CAN! SNICKER!
YOU HAVE TO GO WHERE THE FANS ARE!
SO TRUE!
WHICH REMINDS ME! IT'LL BE SPLITSVILLE AGAIN FOR US AFTER THIS TOUR!
I KNOW! I KNOW!
2

THE PUSSYCATS SOLO TOUR BEGINS!
AND I HAVE TO GO BACK TO HIGH SCHOOL!
WHY DID I HAVE TO FALL IN LOVE WITH AN OLDER WOMAN?
I'M 3 YEARS OLDER! WHAT'S THE BIG DEAL?
I GUESS THAT MAKES YOU A COUGAR! YOU EVEN HAVE THE COSTUME FOR IT!
GET THIS ON TAPE, RAJ!
MY GOAL IS TO GET SOME HUMILIATING FOOTAGE OF CHERYL!
I CAN DREAM...
3

WOW! VANCOUVER HAS ALL KINDS OF FILMING GOING ON!
VANCOUVER IS OTHERWISE KNOWN AS HOLLYWOOD NORTH!
BECAUSE OF ITS ECONOMICAL ADVANTAGE, MANY SHOWS AND MOVIES FILM HERE!
I LOVE IT! IT'S SO PEACEFUL...
WHAT DO YOU MEAN...
IN INDIA I'M A HUGE STAR! I GET FOLLOWED EVERYWHERE!
BUT HERE, I'M BARELY RECOGNIZED!
OH, I'M SORRY.
OH, DON'T GET ME WRONG! I LOVE IT!
YOU DO?
IT FEELS GOOD TO BE WITH PEOPLE MY AGE! TO HANG OUT... AND BE NORMAL!
4

WOW! IF YOU THINK WE'RE NORMAL, YOU NEED HELP!
YOU'RE ALWAYS WELCOME TO HANG WITH US ANYTIME!
THANK YOU!
I HATE TO BREAK THIS UP, BUT WE HAVE A SHOW IN AN HOUR!
SO...
WE'RE REALLY ROCKIN' ROGERS ARENA!
AND ARCHIE AND AMISHA SOUND AS SWEET AS EVER!
The Archies
AFTER THE SHOW...
TIME TO GET SOME SHUT EYE!
WE'RE OFF TO CALGARY TOMORROW!
WHY SO SAD, AMISHA?
5

Oh, I'M NOT SAD! I'M HAPPY!
HAPPY THAT I GOT TO MEET YOU ALL!
MY NEW FRIENDS! I HOPE WE STAY THIS WAY!
OF COURSE, AMISHA!
WE'RE ALWAYS YOUR FRIENDS! THAT'S THE RIVERDALE WAY!
I SENSE AMISHA DOESN'T HAVE A LOT OF FRIENDS BACK HOME!
SHE'S BEEN A STAR SINCE SHE WAS A LITTLE GIRL!
SHE DOESN'T HAVE WHAT ALL OF YOU HAVE...
...A NORMAL TEEN-AGE LIFE!
WOW! YOU KNOW, WE REALLY TAKE THINGS FOR GRANTED SOME-TIMES!
6

SOMETIMES JUST HAVING FRIENDS WHO CARE ABOUT YOU IS EVERY-THING!
FWAP
AND SOMETIMES WE'RE STUCK WITH BUFFOONS WHO NEED TO BE TAKEN DOWN! PREPARE TO DIE, DOOFUS!
HA!
HA!
HA!
HA! HA!
CALGARY!
WOW! IT LOOKS LIKE THE WILD WEST OUT HERE!
CALGARY IS HOME TO THE CALGARY STAMPEDE!
AND JUST LOOK AT THOSE ROCKY MOUNTAINS!

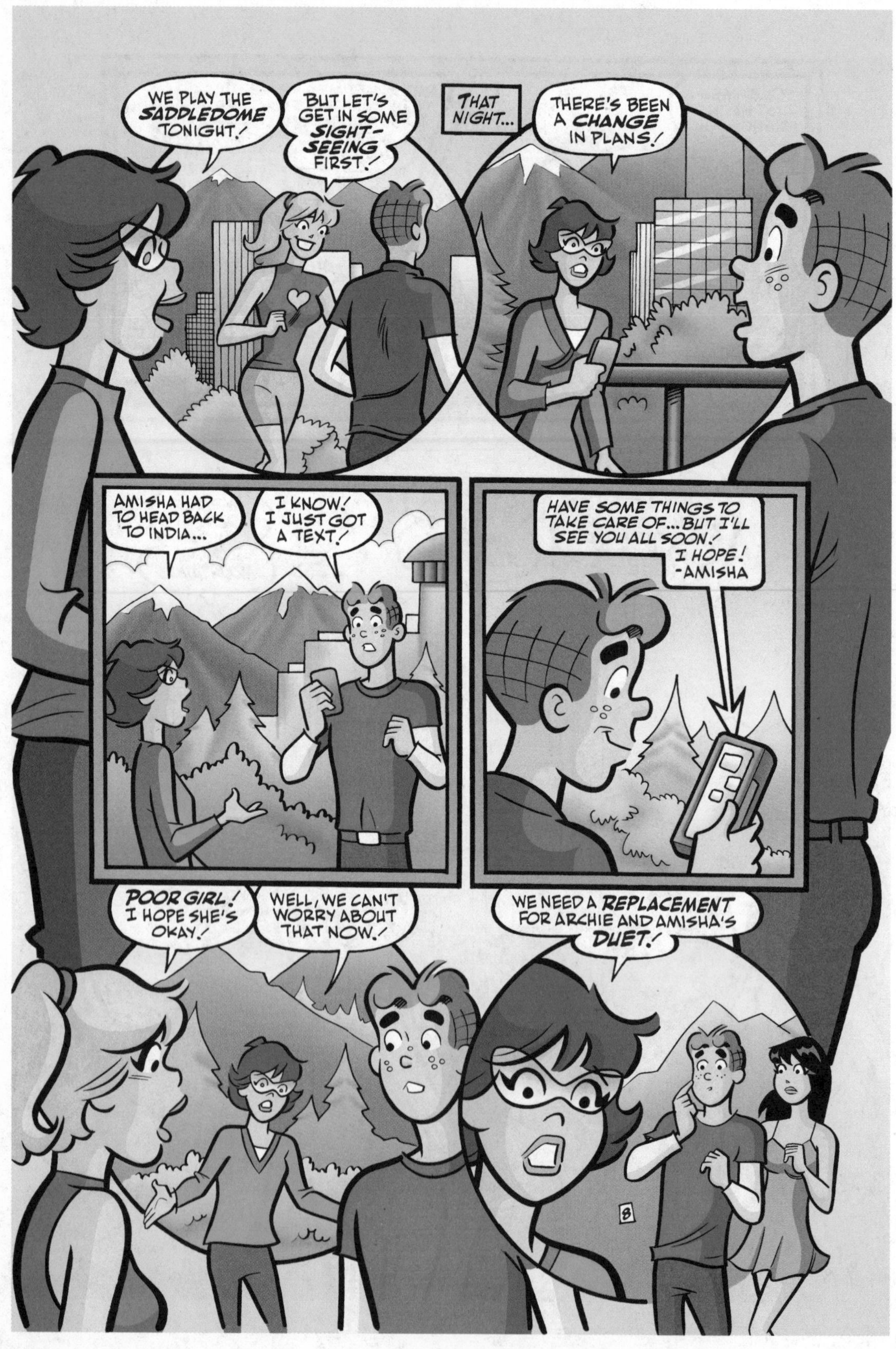
WE PLAY THE SADDLEDOME TONIGHT!
BUT LET'S GET IN SOME SIGHT-SEEING FIRST!
THAT NIGHT...
THERE'S BEEN A CHANGE IN PLANS!
AMISHA HAD TO HEAD BACK TO INDIA...
I KNOW! I JUST GOT A TEXT!
HAVE SOME THINGS TO TAKE CARE OF... BUT I'LL SEE YOU ALL SOON! I HOPE! -AMISHA
POOR GIRL! I HOPE SHE'S OKAY!
WELL, WE CAN'T WORRY ABOUT THAT NOW!
WE NEED A REPLACEMENT FOR ARCHIE AND AMISHA'S DUET!
8

NO TIME TO FLY IN BRIGITTE OR ANYONE ELSE!
IT'LL HAVE TO BE SOMEONE HERE!
I HAVE A SUGGESTION!
WHAT A SURPRISE!
SO!
THIS IS IT! OUR TIME TO SHINE!
YOU'RE GOING TO DO THE DUET WITH ARCHIE!
REALLY? HOW?!
WHEN VALERIE GOES TO CHANGE INTO HER OUTFIT FOR THE DUET--
--I'LL SEE THAT SHE STAYS PUT!
THE YOU RUN OUT AND SAVE THE DAY.!!
PLUS, IT'LL GIVE THIS BORING DOCUMENTARY THE KICK IN THE PANTS THAT IT NEEDS!
9

FINALLY! I'LL BE A STAR! GRAMMY AWARDS, WATCH OUT!
UH... TAKE IT DOWN A NOTCH, ALEXANDRIA!
THAT NIGHT!
YOU'RE UP NEXT, VALERIE!
OKAY! GOTTA CHANGE FROM PUSSY-CAT...
...TO SEXY CHANTEUSE!
NOW, I'VE GOT TO...
HEY! THE DOOR IS LOCKED!
I'D BETTER CALL FOR HELP...
I'LL TAKE THAT!
CHERYL! WHAT ARE YOU UP TO NOW?!
IT'S TIME FOR YOU TO TAKE A BACK SEAT, SISTER!
WHO'S GONNA MAKE ME?!
10

SHOVE
GET IN THIS CLOSET!!
WE'RE STAYING IN HERE UNTIL ARCHIE AND ALEX'S MUSICAL NUMBER IS OVER!
ALEXANDRA?! SHE CAN'T SING! SHE'LL MAKE A MOCKERY OF THE WHOLE SHOW!!
HA! WE AUTO-TUNED AND PRE-RECORDED HER PART FOR HER TO LIPSYNC! AND WE KNOW THAT AUTO-TUNE CAN MAKE A HOWLING COYOTE SOUND GOOD...!
SO...
WHERE IS SHE?! ARCHIE'S SWEATING BULLETS!!
HE NEEDS HELP UP THERE!
POOR GUY!
I'M HERE TO...
I'LL HELP OUT!!
11

OMIGOSH! IT'S CANADIAN SUPERSTAR CELINE DIJON!
WHAT A COINCIDENCE THAT YOU HAPPEN TO BE HERE!
I'M A HUGE FAN! MAY I?
YOU BETCHA!
♫ AND YOUR LOVE IS SO REAL...
IT SOUNDS GREAT FROM HERE!
THAT DOESN'T SOUND LIKE ALEXANDRA!
WAH!
CHERYL! OPEN UP!!
WHAT'S GOING ON?!
WHAT HAPPENED?!
I WAS PUSHED ASIDE BY NONE OTHER THAN CELINE DIJON!!
12

WHAT?! CAN'T YOU DO ANYTHING RIGHT?!!
HONESTLY! AM I THE ONLY ONE WITH A BRAIN HERE?!
YOU BOOBS! ONLY YOU TWO COULD IMPROVE THE CONCERT BY ACCIDENT!
WOW! THEY SOUND GREAT!!
A STANDING OVATION!
WAY TO GO, CHERYL!
IT WAS AN HONOR TO SING WITH YOU!
VALERIE! WHAT HAPPENED?
IT'S A LONG STORY!
BUT A GOOD ONE!
SNICKER!
NEXT STOP, MONTREAL!
Oh, HOW I LOVE THIS CULTURAL OLD CITY!
13

IT'S OLD ARCHITECTURE IS SO BEAUTIFUL! ESPECIALLY IN THE "OLD MONTREAL" SECTION!
BONJOUR! COMMENT CA VA AUJOURD'HUI?
AND THE FACT THAT FRENCH IS SPOKEN HERE PRIMARILY IS SO SEXY!
I LIKE THE POUTAIN!
THAT NIGHT AT THE BELL CENTRE...
ARCHIE AND VALERIE! YOU WERE GREAT!
WELL, I'M NO CELINE DIJON, BUT...
Hmm... WHAT'S WRONG?
I JUST REALIZED...
...WE ONLY HAVE ONE CONCERT LEFT... IN TORONTO...
YEAH...
14

THEN IT'S BACK TO SCHOOL...
AND BACK ON THE ROAD...
LET'S NOT GET TOO DEPRESSED! WE HAVE TO GIVE IT OUR BEST YET!
IN TORONTO!
NOTHING LIKE BEING IN CANADA'S BIGGEST CITY!
THERE'S NO VIEW OF TORONTO LIKE THE ONE FROM THE CN TOWER!
YOU CAN SAY THAT AGAIN!
The BINGOS! AND The GLADS!
WE'RE HERE FOR THE GRAND FINALE!
IT WOULDN'T BE THE SAME WITHOUT YOU GUYS!
15

TELL US ABOUT YOUR OWN TOUR!
WE WOULDN'T HAVE BEEN NOTICED IF IT WASN'T FOR THIS TOUR!
HOW CAN WE EVER THANK YOU?
HOW ABOUT PUTTING ON A GREAT SHOW TONIGHT!
DEAL!!
THAT NIGHT, AT THE AIR CANADA CENTRE!
AND THAT ENDS OUR ROCKIN' WORLD TOUR!
THANKS TO EVERYONE FOR SUPPORTING US!
AND THERE'S JUST ONE THING LEFT FOR US TO DO FOR ALL OF YOU--
16

GROUP JAM!!
SUGAR SUGAR
AWW HONEY HONEY!
Josie and the PUSSY CATS
HOORAY!
YOU ROCK!
YAY!
GO BABY!
WOW! THAT'S IT! I'M SAD!
I'M RELIEVED!
I NEED A NAP!
MY WORK BEGINS NOW! I HAVE HUNDREDS OF HOURS OF FOOTAGE TO POUR THROUGH FOR THE DOCUMENTARY!
17

YOU'LL DO IT AGAIN! THIS IS JUST THE BEGINNING...
SABRINA! HOW DID YOU GET HERE?
YOU ALWAYS SHOW UP UNEXPECTEDLY!
YEAH, HOW ABOUT THAT?
BACK IN RIVER-DALE...
WELL, RED! HERE WE ARE AGAIN!
I HAVE TO HIT THE ROAD...
AND YOU HAVE TO HIT THE BOOKS!
SIGH! HOW DEPRESSING!
YOU'RE IN GOOD HANDS! YOU'VE GOT THE GANG!
YEAH...
WE'LL BE TOGETHER SOON!
VALERIE...
18

...DON'T FALL IN LOVE WITH ANYONE ELSE!
I COULD SAY THE SAME TO YOU!
WE'RE YOUNG! WE HAVE TO REALIZE THINGS CAN HAPPEN...
...BUT AT THE SAME TIME...
...NOBODY COMPARES TO YOU!
I LOVE YOU, VALERIE!
I REALLY, REALLY LOVE YOU!
YOU SOUND SURPRISED!
I THINK I AM!
SMOOCH!
19

EPILOGUE:
ARCHIE!!
WE HAVE A NEW STUDENT HERE AT RIVERDALE HIGH!
NONE OTHER THAN...
AMISHA MEHTA!!
WHAT?! THAT'S AWESOME! BUT HOW? WHAT ABOUT INDIA? YOUR CAREER?
YOU ALL MADE ME REALIZE THE IMPORTANCE OF FRIENDSHIP!
AND THAT I WANT A NORMAL TEEN-AGE LIFE FOR AWHILE!
I CAN'T HAVE ANONYMITY IN INDIA... BUT I CAN HERE!
I FEEL SO WELCOME HERE ALREADY!
THAT'S WHAT HAPPENS HERE IN RIVERDALE! EVERYBODY'S WELCOME HERE!
WELCOME TO RIVERDALE, AMISHA!
END